The Web

Stories by Argentine Women

Edited and Translated by H. Ernest Lewald

© H. Ernest Lewald 1983

First Edition
Three Continents Press
1346 Connecticut Ave. N.W.
Washington, D.C. 20036

🅣🅢🅟

ISBN 0-89410-085-8; -086-6 (pbk)
LC No. 81-51646

Cover Art by Maryse Dejean

The Web

Acknowledgements

I wish to give my heartfelt thanks to Norma Lee Eden for her help in translating *El amante* and *La niña Panchita* and her encouragement to produce this volume of stories by Argentine women writers.

I gratefully express my appreciation to the authors and institutions listed below who granted permission to publish the following selections translated into English by me:

Silvina Bullrich for *Abnegación* and *El amante* from *Historias inmorales.*

Marta Lynch for *Cuentos de colores* and *Campo de batalla.*

Beatriz Guido for *Diez vueltas a la manzana* and *Piel de verano* from *La mano en la trampa.*

Luisa Mercedes Levinson for *El abra* and *La niña Panchita* from *La pálida rosa de Soho.*   '

Syria Poletti for *El último pecado* from *Línea de fuego.*

Maria Angélica Bosco for *De María Angélica Bosco a Esther Vilar* in *Cartas de mujeres.*

Editorial Sur for *La oración* from *La furia* by Silvina Ocampo.

Luisa Valenzuela for *Cambio de guardia.*

Eugenia Calny for *Siesta* from *Las mujeres virtuosas.*

Amalia Jamilis for *Las grandes tiendas* and *Los trabajos nocturnos.*

Cecilia Absatz for *Un ballet para las bailarinas* from *Feiguele y otras mujeres.*

Reina Roffé for *Oigamos lo que tenga que decir.*

Contents

Introduction

The River Plate countries, Argentina and Uruguay, belong to a continent that for many present-day geopoliticians forms part of the amorphous under– or semi-developed conglomeration of nations known as the Third World. Yet, Argentines and Uruguayans would quickly reject such a classification. They will quote statistics that show them to have the most literate, best-fed, largest middle class with the highest income and the lowest birth rate of Latin America. Walking through the Parisian boulevards of downtown Buenos Aires with its world-famous Colon Opera House, the elegant Barrio Norte, four subway lines, the sidewalk cafes, bistros and boutiques, London's Harrods, the Roman traffic jams, one has the impression of being in a European capital. A similar claim can be made about Montevideo across the River Plate, the Mediterranean-looking capital of Uruguay that resembles Barcelona or Marseilles.

But Buenos Aires also is *La cabeza de Goliat,* as the Argentine essayist Martinez Estrada put it, the monstrous head of a country filled with empty and endless pampas, jungles to the subtropical North in Misiones and frozen tundras to the South in Patagonia. One of three Argentines lives in Greater Buenos Aires, a city of over eight million people in 1980. All the cultural media are concentrated here: publishing houses, magazines, the television and film industries, theater life and art exhibits. The number of book stores and art galleries rivals that of Paris or London. Practically all writers and artists live and work within a thirty-mile radius of the heart of the city; and blind Jorge Luis Borges crossing the street from his apartment on Maipú Street to the Galeria del Este to sit and chat in his favorite bookstore every afternoon lends a charming note to the perfectly cosmopolitan ambiance.

Yet, Argentina is not a fully industrialized or developed nation. The pampas that begin beyond the last suburban high-rise apartment building

3

are for the most part empty with the exception of a few manufacturing centers like Córdoba and Rosario. The Spaniards had paid little attention to the rolling prairies since they were looking for a massive Indian labor force and precious metals. The River Plate area offered neither and thus remained unexploited until waves of European immigrants began to hit Buenos Aires and Montevideo after 1870. Thus millions of Italians and Spaniards, and large numbers of Irish, Germans, Eastern European Jews and Syrians arrived around the turn of the century, descending from the ships in search of the riches of Eldorado. These immigrants brought their special European heritage of literacy, crafts and a nineteenth century awareness of class struggle and economic justice. They also shared a burning desire to create a better life for their children. These factors merged later in the decade of 1945-1955 when that singular couple, Juan and Evita Perón, took up the cause of the *descamisados,* the shirtless proletariat, and opposed the ruling landed gentry as well as its supporters in the armed forces and the Catholic Church.

Culturally, the dominant tone was set by the Mediterranean legacy, the combined influence of the Hispanic and Italian system of values and mores that included a sexual double standard. As the elitist colonial mentality of the nineteenth century gave way to the trends of a mass industrialized society in the twentieth century, the existing political, social and economic system became gradually modified. Labor unrest slowly forced laissez-faire capitalism to modify its sweatshop tactics; populist pressures brought about secret-ballot voting after 1890; Buenos Aires sent socialist representatives and senators to Congress; and in 1947 Evita Perón gave women the right to vote. As immigration subsided, Argentine culture achieved some measure of cohesion and the descendants of the European arrivals an Argentine Spanish with a heavy dose of Italian vocabulary. They often outdid the *criollos viejos,* the proud old "colonials," at the game of nationalism. But as the capital slowly evolved into a metropolis, the multitudes felt an increasing sense of anonymity and alienation common to any big city in our era.

Throughout the history of this growth, the destiny of the female inhabitant, *la porteña,* underwent corresponding changes. From a fairly serene and sheltered existence in the post-colonial *gran aldea* or big village in the nineteenth century, she hastily retreated under a state of masculine siege as the ships docking in the New Port let loose hundreds of thousands of adventurous young males who began to roam the streets in search of a suitable female. Not surprisingly, Buenos Aires earned the ill repute of being the world's center of white slavery where naive European girls, having signed up to become performing "artists," found themselves chained to an iron bed post. Manuel Gálvez's best seller of 1919, *Nacha Regules,* portrays a vicious, sex-starved Buenos Aires covered with the red lights of thousands of brothels where the sensual, slow music of the tango was born.

The fact that the men outnumbered the women combined with the Don Juan syndrome deeply imbedded in the Mediterranean culture, proved to be an enormous obstacle to achieving a balanced relationship between the sexes.

In the 1930's, Swiss-born Alfonsina Storni, the first important feminist writer of Argentina, tearfully complained to the police prefect about male sexual rapacity on the streets of downtown Buenos Aires. Not surprisingly, she wrote in her most celebrated poem: "Little man, let me out of your cage/I loved you half an hour/don't ask me for more." Much of her work repeats this grave accusation: the Argentine male can only approach a woman in the role of a seducer. In the case of marriage, the female sex object must also take on other functions such as bearing children, playing the perfect mother and being an inspiration to the family and society at large as an example of virtue while the husband was entirely free to establish his proverbial *casa chica,* a home away from home with a younger woman.

During the 1950's and 1960's the number of males to females had evened out somewhat, and the ranks of the middle classes had been swelled by the upward mobility of the descendants of lower-class immigrants. However, the young men in Bernardo Verbitsky's novels and stories who populate the cafés and streetcorners of Buenos Aires still saw woman as the antagonist, an unknown entity that, if they were lucky, would become a conquest, seldom a companion. The middle-class males, often professionals now, had internalized the earlier cultural norms dominating female-male relationships. The bourgeois woman found herself in the role of a married woman dependent both economically and psychologically on her husband. Her frustration usually began when her role as a desirable, young wife changed into that of a mother and matron. She must accept her husband's sexual escapades and liaisons with the resignation of someone who was not able to fend for herself in an alien world, much less apply for a very difficult to obtain divorce.

It was in this period that a number of Argentine women writers began to write about the frustration, anger and fatalism of their captive sisters. In the early novels and stories of Silvina Bullrich, Marta Lynch and Maria Angélica Bosco, the heroines suffer, endure and at times rebel by taking a

6

lover to help their self image; seldom do they slam the door to Nora's "doll house."

In the present decade the *porteña* began to realize that the prerequisite to personal freedom was economic self-sufficiency. Thus the mammoth University of Buenos Aires today enrolls more women than men and the female night-school students in Reina Roffé's recently banned novel *Monte de Venus* (1976) try to obtain a High School diploma by seducing their male professors. But *porteña* society is still a combat zone in which the male exacts his tribute from any female who wants to climb the ladder of success in a male-dominated world, be it advertising, television or motion pictures. Sexual exploitation, mistrust and alienation still pervade a good deal of male-female relationships, and the Argentine feminine writer records the struggle in detail. Only too often have these relationships been explored from a male writer's point of view. It would be impossible to produce a synoptic picture of female-male attitudes as seen by the male Argentine writer, but it is fairly certain that none of these authors would have echoed the words of Silvina Bullrich's heroine in her recent novel, *Te acordarás de Taormina,* when she ironically exclaims: "I don't know whether to enter domestic bliss or become a prostitute. It's a difficult choice."

The women writers included in this anthology constitute a representative cross-section of the present-day *porteña* whose fiction portrays her urban society and culture with the main focus on the constantly changing problems in female-male relationships. A majority of them have been writing for quite a long time and, like Silvina Bullrich and Beatriz Guido, have produced a large number of novels and stories. A few, like Amalia Jamilis and Luisa Valenzuela, belong to a newer generation. The youngest, Reina Roffé, show that there exists continuity and promise in the future of Argentine feminist prose. All of them make their home in Greater Buenos Aires, many of them travel frequently throughout the Americas and Europe, most are well acquainted with French, English and American literature, often in the original, and some have written books that have outsold their male colleagues' best efforts.

While a good deal of their fiction is concerned with other social issues—political ones at times—or constitutes an attempt at experimental writing, all of them have produced works that show their awareness of being a woman writing in a complex and very dynamic culture. Some of their best prose is found in novels, and this precluded their inclusion in this anthology. The stories and the essay selected for this anthology, however, hopefully provide an authentic picture of women in a unique Hispanic society whose feminist voices can now be heard for the first time by the North American public.

H. E. Lewald

LUISA MERCEDES LEVINSON

Born in 1914 in Buenos Aires, Luisa Mercedes Levinson is a descendant of English and Spanish families. During her long career she has written novels, short stories and a few plays. Cosmopolitan in spirit and a traveler by inclination, she feels equally at home in London, San Francisco, Buenos Aires or on a Greek island. Her association with Jorge Luis Borges has resulted in a volume of stories, *La hermana de Eloisa.* But his influence is also visible in some of the stories of the volume *Las tejedoras sin hombre* and in the more recent novel *A la sombra del buho* in which Levinson manipulates time, space and the perception of reality much in the manner of Borges, the admirer of Berkeley and Schopenhauer.

But unlike most of the Argentine women writers, who prefer to remain within the spatial and social context of the River Plate, Levinson has found inspiration in the somewhat exotic milieu of the subtropical Northern Argentine province of Entrerrios that she came to know so well while living there on her father's estate. Witnessing the sway of an exuberant and at times hostile nature over the local inhabitants, she captured the primitive spirit that too often forced women into the role of victim of a brutal male environment.

Her stories dealing with this rural environment—considered among her best by most Argentine critics—are, however, far from being simple naturalistic accounts. Rather, the author is interested in exploring the mental processes of her female characters as they confront an overwhelming *machista* possessiveness. The prostitute in "The Clearing"

9

and the branded girl in "Mistress Frances" are among the best examples of this theme.

BIBLIOGRAPHY

La casa de los Felipe, 1951 (novel)

La hermana de Eloisa (in collaboration with Jorge Luis Borges), 1955 (stories)

Concierto en mi, 1956 (novel)

La palida rosa de Soho, 1962 (stories)

La isla de los organilleros, 1964 (novel)

Las tejedoras sin hombre, 1967 (stories)

A la sombra del buho, 1972 (novel)

La estigma del tiempo, 1977 (stories)

The Clearing

Luisa Mercedes Levinson

In the midst of the clearing, half overrun by vegetation, on the land belonging to the Basque Mendihondo, stands a miserable shack consisting of two rooms, a porch and a zinc roof that the tropical sun was trying to melt.

The clearing, about a mile in diameter, was surrounded by the jungle of Misiones in northern Argentina, a primeval force that threatened to strangle the open space with its green noose. The clearing looked like a dry island crossed only by some ostriches or monkeys or, once in a great while, by an errant Indian who, like myself, was running away from his own poverty by venturing out into the jungle and the red desert.

At one time the shack wore a coat of white paint and a few cows grazed on the clearing. A deep water well with a mule tied to the *noria* provided the only source of water. From the high beams on the porch hung a Paraguayan-style hammock, and stretched out in it lay the body of a copper-skinned woman with short but well-rounded limbs who was cooling herself with a fan made out of reeds. In spite of her dark skin she did not look like a local girl; the exaggerated use of kohl made her eyes look exotic. The flimsy dress accentuated the heavy outline of her body. The hammock swayed a little, weighed down by the compact figure. An amorphous vapour hung about her like a halo, but it just might have been an ondulating cloud of mosquitos.

The boss, Alcibiades, had brought her one night when returning from Oberá, and she had stayed on. He never called her by her name, only: "Hey, say, look." She had a name that was difficult to pronounce. She had thought that this bearded stranger with the expressionless eyes, limber movements and the gaucho belt covered with silver coins, would take her to cities where the ferris wheels at the fair would lift her up to the sky or where music can be heard from a distance while the bottle made its round

11

among the men at sundown.

But they just stayed on the clearing without as much as a dog or a guitar. Then the man hired Ciro to be the peon. Ciro watered the cattle, he castrated and skinned animals, prepared food, served mate tea and washed the clothes. He also carried the hammock from one end of the porch to the other in search of shade, sometimes with the woman inside of the net. He seldom spoke, At night he squatted next to the porch pillar, unobtrusive and silent. Since he did not smoke, his face remained invisible. His eyes shone although not as brightly as the stars in the deep night.

In the dark Alcibiades threw away his cigarette butt and approached the hammock. He stood there for quite a while; suddenly he picked up the woman and carried her to his room.

Early in the morning Ciro prepared the mate in the gourd. The woman was back in the hammock as if she had never left it, fanning herself without stopping, fresh kohl around her eyes. The expression on her face equalled that worn by many women in the subtropical land: a mask depicting melancholia or tedium, and behind the mask, nothing.

Ciro served her the mate gourd from his crouched position on the red earth; he also offered her cigars made of dried corn leaves, fruits or sometimes a partridge that he had caught at a lake fifteen miles from there. The boss looked at them from the shack while putting on his belt with the silver pieces. The boy certainly was a hard worker and he had come to like him.

One morning while the woman was eating fruit from some far-away palm trees, she spotted a rattle snake. She shot its head off as she had done so many times with the gun that she kept in the hammock.

That brought out Alcibiades. "Hey, good shot. You deserve something for that aim of yours. I'm going to town and taking a few steers along. I'll bring you a blouse."

"You want me to come along, boss?" asked Ciro.

"No."

Alcibiades pointed at the gun. "There's one bullet left. That should be enough for you."

He left. The mask in the hammock remained unchanged.

Ciro mounted the mare and made his usual rounds; he brought three straying cows back from the jungle, he wormed a calf, cured the scabies and scraped the larvae off others and mended the wooden fence. When he returned to the shack, he began his domestic chores; he started a fire to barbecue some meat while the wind was blowing dust in his face. Stooped over the red earth he shot a glance at the woman. She stretched and then began to unbutton her blouse as if the buttons were constricting her chest. She continued to lie in the hammock fanning herself while the face remained completely expressionless; only her body seemed to be swaying in the net, shimmering like so many multi-colored fish twisting and turning in the monstrous deep. She exuded sparks of a remote and yet aggressive sort of beauty. Ciro, still on his knees, moved slowly and silently closer to the woman and began to caress the hand hanging down from the hammock. Her hand moved up to the breast carrying along Ciro's hand. Ciro jumped onto the net, feverish and desperate, the blood singing in his veins. His warm sweat ran into a deep, female saltiness; the woman opened her lips wide. A milky peacefulness settled on the lonely reddish earth from which even the birds had departed. Suddenly the woman's cry broke the silence, and Ciro's body fell onto the hard ground underneath the hammock.

"Didn't expect me back so soon now, did you? At least I didn't make him bleed all over you, you should thank me for that."

Alcibiades came closer, shoved the revolver under his belt and began to use his lassoo like a thread, sewing up the net from top to bottom. The woman lay very still, completely quiet, her eyes wide open without actually looking at anything while the rope was closing the net over her face and body. He concentrated hard on his work and very neatly tied the rope into a final double knot over her feet.

She still did not realize what had happened. The rope lay across her face and cut into her breasts. A scent rose from the ground, a mixture of gun powder and sex and other things that seemed far away and hidden. Contorting her body she made the hammock swing and her face turned to the ground. There lay the dead body: a bullet had shattered the forehead, the nose looked slightly crooked, and the mouth represented a sweet and grateful wound, the lips of a boy who had just been kissed.

The woman's senses were still dulled by the apparent peacefulness that gradually ebbed away. She did not understand how fear worked. She only knew that what was to come could hardly be worse than what had been before. She had touched bottom a long time ago. Happiness for her would never be more than a confused memory of a fleeting moment. A little while ago she had come to know a profound joy, possibly for the first time; and, in spite of what had just happened, a wave of well-being invaded her, pushing aside reality and transporting her in time, keeping her locked in a present that no longer existed. In the whorehouse of Doña Jacinta she had come to know the need of many men, but nothing ever happened to make her recover the preciousness of remote things: her childhood, a ship, a certain song. Her breasts and belly began to weigh her down like some gigantic rocks. She opened her eyes. Ciro was but a quiet, elongated figure on the ground. As she twisted in the net a stony, grey hatred that seemed to have seeped out of the red earth began to inundate and overwhelm her. Scraping her hips she managed to turn sideways. Her hatred had nothing to do with the anguish or frustration of finding herself humiliated, a prisoner caught in the roped net. Her hatred was directed against the man who represented power and oppression, the boss, Alcibiades, standing next to the pillar, the very same place that had given shelter to hope, patience, poverty and love: Ciro's place.

The woman's face had become a mask again. But behind it she relived a scene from the past when the bearded man had appeared in Doña Jacinta's patio late one afternoon, his boots squeaking, his heavy figure eclipsing the light as he looked over the girls: Zoila, so fragile that she seemed on the verge of breaking in two, Wilda with her kinky hair, thick lips and greenish eyes, and all the others. And then he had picked her and made her lie down with her hands clutching her neck, and a wave of revulsion had risen in her, something that never happened before. Then he promised to take her to the big cities and plied her with corn-leaf cigars, and she forgot her loathing and went with him, leaving a heap of clothes for the other girls. She was going to get a brand new outfit, even real light-blue silken underwear. And then they ended up at the clearing, and life was not better than in that patio, and the days went by, nothing changed, dawn turned into dusk and night into day, and always the same heat.

The hatred was choking her now, erupting deep inside of her, similar to her revulsion when Alcibiades had kissed her for the first time as she arched her back. Something dormant within her, like a stagnant pond, was spilling over her mind and body, sweeping along incongruent, astonishing images. She felt now cleansed from all previous contamination, lucid and determined to carry out her revenge. She could hear him walking around inside, counting his silver coins, opening a suitcase and putting clothes and the poncho from the bed in it. He was leaving her, leaving her to be sucked up by the sun that was about to hit the porch while a cloud of greenish, sticky flies zoomed up to her from the bloody head on the ground. Far away the buzzards and crows were waiting. Her tongue felt like straw and her stomach was growing a hundred claws, but she was not conscious of suffering hunger pains or, above all, thirst. Her hatred had erased everrything else. A soft smell arose from the ground. It was a sweetish smell, not unlike that produced by two sweaty bodies in the act of making love.

Alcibiades, suitcase in hand, stopped next to the pillar, a sort of grin spreading over his taut lips. He did not quite know how to measure the consequences of his act, but in a way he admired himself for his decision. He had killed a man, the boy, and he had clearly gotten rid of something that bothered him. Now he had to flee. That was a bother too, and he did not quite know what to do next. It was hot and time to take a siesta.

The woman looked like a jaguar, short limbs and a bulky chest and belly, reddish spots appearing on her skin under the sun-flooded net. Her body started to twist. The sun was hitting her right shoulder and hip. She had turned her back to the dead body and the sun shone on her heavy breast partly covered by the rope. A purplish nipple was sticking out through one of the squares of the net. Her abundant hair was spread over her face and barely allowed her eyes to shine through. She began to let out a repetitious, hoarse moan; it sounded a little like a lullaby. At the same time an instinctive knowledge arose from somewhere within and filtered through to her brain. All she had to do was to utter the right sounds and the man would come closer, throw himself on her, undo the knot and slip out the rope, and the hammock would open up. It would also mean the triumph of the female; and life, power and revenge would be hers.

Alcibiades acted ill at ease standing next to the pillar. He put the suitcase down, came a step closer and stopped.

"Hey, that sun is roasting you," he said in a strange, thick voice.

Her body began to twist again and she let out a groan. He spoke slowly now, as if he had trouble getting the words out: "Now nobody will bother us, not even the sun."

He was coming closer, stopping and starting again. She saw his body growing, towering. Any moment now he would make the final jump. Maybe in his hurry he would cut the knot with his hunting knife.

The twisting of the woman's body had changed its pace; there was a new trembling that the man failed to notice. The hatred hit her in successive, quick waves, taking over, conquering her shrewdness, her indolence, her physical needs, all that she had been until now. The waves of boiling hatred engulfed her total being. Her hatred was more impatient and impulsive than his lust. Her awareness of self-preservation was being swept away, her revenge could wait no longer. The feeling of hatred had become ferocious, tyrannical, all-consuming. She could no longer stop it . .
. . . the gun in her hand went off.

"Bitch," mumbled the man through his clenched teeth. His body turned and fell backwards onto the ground. He clutched his chest with one hand while spitting out some confused oaths.

In the hammock the revolver remained empty, useless. This had been the last bullet, the last roar to break the hum, the heaviness and the thirst. It was the last noise of the world to reach her. That man, Alcibiades, stretched out on the ground, his body still trembling, loomed darkly, like a shadow against the light, swearing and dying. And finally, it was all over, death under the pillar, next to the bulging, old suitcase. A thread of blood was making a design on the grimy, whitish shirt partly hidden by the black beard.

The woman now yielded herself to the sun that possessed her completely. Now that her hatred had been stilled, it abandoned her—like a man—she became submerged in a sort of opaque, profound peace, a sense of peace very much like the one she had experienced as an aftermath of her love-making. But this new peace was going to be endless.

Bearing down on the red earth of the clearing the sun was concentrating with tenacity on the humid body under the net that was drying up little by little. The buzzing cloud of flies moved from the sun into the shade and back, settling on the bodies of the dead men and then on her, without making any distinction between the punctured forehead, the oozing blood on the chest and her thirsty body. Her hatred had been kept alive at the expense of the thirst, and something inside of her had been fulfilled, sated. For a while she lay there, drowsy. Suddenly she bit into the net with despair. One little square broke, then another. Her skin, her eyelids and her lips were on fire. Everything around her was burning although night was falling, as heavy as a hundred men on top of her. The jungle came to life at a distance, crawling at first, then galloping furiously, closing in on the clearing, strangling it. She was blinded by the reflection of far-away lakes and treacherous rivers that advanced and retreated. Night, sun, night again. She gnawed at the threads of fear and solitude. Her own screams engendered silent echoes that took on shapes, surrounded her, scared her, and thundered on into the night. Then silence enveloped her and the lassoo's knot over her feet grew larger, unreachable, all-powerful.

The jungle rushes onwards. Shadows, sticky wings slap her face, beaks peck at her thighs and hips, splattering her with blackness and death:

"Wilda and Zoila are asleep under the mosquito net. The customers are here! Doña Jacinta is going to get angry. My legs are caught in a vine, and the men's hands are squeezing the girls' breasts filled with a yellow and bitter milk to deceive the men's thirst. Little mother! My entrails are on fire. The palm trees and the snakes are burning. Down below the silver coins and the black beard are consumed by the fire; everything is a brakish liquid . . .

"Wheels rolling through towns. Ciro, Ciro, cut me loose from this wheel! There below, in the patio filled with jasmine, stand the soldiers in their pretty blue uniforms. And angels fly through the air singing. He is bringing silk blouses for all the girls. Let's all pray to the Virgin for a miracle: pretty underwear and a man around the house. The jungle is covering me, hiding me in its leaves. Vegetation, jungle . . . little Virgin, air creature, don't blind me with your light . . . "

The hammock, suspended in midair like a bridge or a murmuring dream, was softly swinging over death when I, the poor Indian traveller, arrived.

Mistress Frances

Luisa Mercedes Levinson

You may remember, Your Honor, that as a young child, Mistress Frances used to come to the ranch with her half-sister. And yet to call her a child isn't really right; she was always so fair and innocent that she seemed like a child. Like as not, it was because of her that the guacho* had a habit of leaving the kitchen and wandering around the houses. It was a bad habit because nobody likes to be stared at—whether you're awake or asleep—especially if you think you're alone. Well, as I said, the guacho used to wander around the houses and sometimes he'd lean his forehead against the glass in the doors, staring with his eyes big as dry wells. Don M. Z. wouldn't stand for anyone trespassing, and whenever he caught the guacho around the house, he'd just go after the boy with a whip. Anyone else would have run away, but not the guacho; he stood his ground, and, of course, Don M. Z. punished the guacho; we used to get a kick out of watching the whole thing from the bunkhouse—the boss used to put on a real show, shouting about disrespect and guachos being worse than hoof and mouth disease!

One morning after the men had left to get the branding done, I saw the guacho from a distance. He was bent over the lintel that overlooks the houses, carving the initials "M. Z." into the wood with a machete. When he saw me, he stood up silently, hiding that look of longing and desire. No more than a week later he left the ranch.

Now, Your Honor, the next important thing is that Miss Frances came out to the ranch that following spring. She was the godchild of Don M. Z.'s dead wife, you know, and she used to sit quietly on the porch with her embroidery; they say she embroidered nothing but "M. Z." on sheets and tablecloths. Don Marcelino Zaldarriaga was an old man and had a fatherly affection for the girl, though some said that wasn't all. But then, people always think bad things about a beautiful girl like Miss Frances with her

18

big eyes, black as charcoal and always half closed and sleepy looking. The most beautiful chinas** around here have always been the girls in the Alzoque family; all of them, even Miss Frances, had a beauty spot right under the ear! Your Honor can appreciate that.

About five years ago a horsebreaker, Abelardo Socas, came to the ranch for the branding season. He used to wander near the M. Z. houses and one night, when he thought everyone was asleep, he approached the houses and Don M. Z. set the dogs on him. It was an odd thing because those dogs always ran around the ranch barking a lot but never hurting anyone. But when dawn came, we found Socas lying there strangled with fang marks on his throat.

From that day on, the ranch wasn't the same. We didn't see Miss Frances on the porch anymore. One day Don M. Z. came back from the rodeo at midday; everyone knows the boss loved rodeos and he always stayed till late night when everything was over, so it seemed strange he came back so soon. He rode in stiff and bent and we put him to bed. He couldn't move his arms. After three days we heard an explosion from his room—he had killed his dog Leal who always slept curled up at the foot of his bed. That night the priest arrived from Macia to give the boss the Last Sacrament. Don Marcelino Zaldarriaga died at dawn.

After Don M. Z. died, no one knew what would happen to Miss Frances. I supposed that she would leave but she never did. Once again she would sit on the porch staring out into the distance, and embroidering "M. Z." on tablecloths and sheets. I never could figure out women.

Well, Your Honor, you already know that the guacho returned after something like six months. He brought presents for everyone, even the new ranch hands. Who would have thought that he was a doctor calling himself Eleutorio Fernández—he came back to fix up the right kind of water holes for the stock. It was because of the ticks that we needed to make new water holes, he said; the M. Z. ranch was at the borderline of the contaminated area, and we had to pass an inspection on the stock and clean out the ticks.

Early on the third day, he went near the houses. Miss Frances was sitting on the porch, like she always did, and she was holding a mburucuyá flower, looking like she was counting the crown of thorns on it. It was the kind of day that makes a man lazy; so, to kill time, I began thinking back on other times. But the only memories I had were bad ones; the boss's blows and his whip, Abelardo Socas, the dog that was killed, and Miss Frances, holding a small candlestick and her shadow, like a giant bat on the wall in her room—her shadow beneath the cross on the wall, behind the other cross on the bars of the grating. I didn't like my memories so I asked permission to go to the kitchen where you can argue and joke all you want and not have to remember bad things alone.

Then, since the guacho had come back, Don M. Z.'s room was called the office; Eleutorio had brought some very large books, a pen and an inkstand that he put on the table. It was hard to guess what Miss Frances thought of all these changes. She continued to be well behaved and innocent looking with her embroidery while Eleutorio wandered about the ranch. If the guacho was the landlord of the M. Z. Ranch, it was no concern of mine. You see, when a man like the guacho takes the cattle to the packing houses and does important things, he still knows he's a guacho and to say landlord is to say that he's as mighty as a mountain or a river! But, when I had to, I went to see him to get my pay even though most of the time I wasted it away as soon as I got it.

But for Eleutorio, confound it, good luck really came his way. He had a knack of giving orders without looking a man in the eye—as if his gaze was only the gaze of a foundling and he was afraid of what you'd see in it. He seemed like he was driven by a more determined force than most other men.

Anyway, after the papers had been signed for the ranch, and Eleutorio was the new landlord, he threw a big party; there was roasted beef, and wine and gin but the mayor didn't come, and, it seemed odd, Miss Frances locked herself up in her room. I was going back to the kitchen when the new boss followed me and nearly stumbled into my arms. Maybe it was the liquor, I'm not sure, but after he got his balance back, he humbled himself to me like an orphan and said that he had suffered so much from being poor and hungry just to become landlord of the M. Z. Ranch. I pulled myself away from him and started to walk away when the guacho began to pout, I guess because Miss Frances had rejected him since he said, "If a ranch is not enough for her, I will give her the boundaries that are all half mortgaged."

Not long after that, we heard that Miss Frances was leaving the ranch. Eleutorio wandered around with a kind of confused look in his eyes and began hanging around the houses. And one day, as I went to the house for my pay, I saw Miss Frances leaning against the door to her room which opened onto the porch. She was beautiful even though she was pale; her coal black eyes seemed to see all the sadness of the land around her. Women should be as fair as she was to make a man's soul warm and to make a man forget his pride and greed. Anyway, Your Honor, suddenly

Eleutorio came up to her, looking at her with longing in his eyes that I never saw before. He knelt down, hid his face in her skirt, and kissed the ruffle on her dress. He said:

"I did it because I wanted to be your equal, because I wanted to marry you, because I love you Miss Frances. Miss Frances, do not drive me away from your side—I will be your slave, your dog. And the ranch I give you, I make you a present of it . . . for nothing . . . Miss Frances . . . ." I drew away because I don't like to hear what only concerns God.

After a short time Eleutorio came to the kitchen, trembling and sweaty; "At dawn go look for the notary public again. Go already! She appears to accept . . . Miss Frances . . . !"

He was an odd fellow; pure enterprise and fearless until the woman he loved came close, then he was the guacho again. A woman should take care of a man so he won't lose control and overflow like a river.

So, my boss had given me a job to do, and that night I got my gear together and was putting it with my saddle so I'd be ready to move out at daybreak when I heard someone quietly walking towards me. I stood very still, holding my breath, in the dark, hoping she wouldn't see me. But she did and she came up to me and just stood there; I could almost smell the blackness of her hair. Maybe she wanted to say something to me, and I wanted her to—I wanted to help her, but I ruined it because I spoke first. "In what way may I serve you, Miss Frances?" and I spoiled everything. Those sparkling eyes that saw so much that the rest of us could not guess! She answered sort of absent-mindedly: "For tomorrow, rope the sorrel of Don M.Z. and leave it saddled here in the paraisos." That was all she said, but she stayed there, like a beautiful statue, gazing into the night till a barn owl screeched and she went back to the house.

At dawn I went to Marciá and engaged the notary public, and by nightfall I was already well on my way back to the M. Z. Ranch. It was one of those really black nights without a moon when the woods seem like a dark herd of cattle without a bell on the lead cow. They say that a man has to whistle when he rides in those woods on a dark night so he'll drive away the souls that roam there. But I wasn't whistling.

A thick mist had begun to rise, seemed like it came to blend the shadows of the dead and the living in those parts. Death must be kind of sad until one gets used to its silence. My grey horse stopped suddenly. Your honor, the voice of a man crept in with the wind. I could make out only one word, "purity" or "you are purity." Afterwards, nothing. Even for the ranch hand the night is long when he is waiting and doesn't know what he is waiting for. Only waiting and nothing more.

A woman's scream pierced the mountain ridges. It was then that my horse began to move and I followed the screams deep into the heart of the woods, straight down through the hawthorns. There in front of me stood two sorrels tied to a carob tree; Don M. Z.'s and the other. I dismounted and took my machete to clear a way through the brush when I heard a man's voice that sounded mean as a rattler's venom:

"Bitch!" he shouted.

There in the cove I saw them. Saw her white back and her, lying face down, saw her quiver in a tremor. That was the last she moved; afterwards there was only that pure white skin on her back and standing out of it was the butt of a knife nailed dead center in the middle of an old scar. A scar made by a branding iron, the same we use on the cattle at the ranch, with the initials "M. Z." burned into her skin.

The other person, or shadow, I saw afterwards; standing there like the trunk of a large tree, dark and silent. Slowly, he knelt down and pulled the knife from that pure white skin. Quietly I overtook him in the darkness . . . I waited a moment . . . then I began to cut with my machete till the shadow of that man fell bleeding to the ground beside her. It was the guacho—the foundling—more a foundling now. I turned my back on him and started to dig. The earth covers white skin. It covers well.

You see, Your Honor, if I didn't speak before, it was because it all comes out the same, whether you believe he did it or I did it. His ghost will fly away from the woods. But mine—that doesn't concern anyone. But, Your Honor, Judge, you shouldn't have dug up what the earth covered. No man should see what your Honor has uncovered. It is too high a price to pay. The dead should be left to rest where first placed. Anyone who has seen the M.Z. brand on Miss Frances' back will always see it no matter if it's on her back, in the mountain ridges and the rivers on the M.Z. ranch, or in her coal black eyes as it always was—because, Your Honor, those letters were branded into my soul.

*guacho   illegitimate country boy in Argentina

**chinas   Quecha Indian term for "low-class" country girls in the Argentine provinces

SILVINA OCAMPO

Silvina Ocampo, born in 1906, belongs to an earlier generation of women writers. Coming from one of Argentina's most aristocratic families, she was afforded the privelege of enjoying the esthetic and intellectual comforts of Europe and Buenos Aires. Her sister Victoria, the first female member of the Argentine Academy of Letters, had been in the center of River Plate literary and cultural activities since the launching of her journal and publishing house *Sur* in 1931. Silvina Ocampo's husband, Adolfo Bioy Casares, is a well known novelist who shares her social background and lifestyle. Throughout her life she felt drawn to the writing of poetry and the translation of French and English authors into her native Spanish. Her penchant for the surreal and magical elements in the narrative motivated her to collaborate with Jorge Luis Borges and her husband in an anthology of Argentine fantastic stories.

Aside from her numerous volumes of poetry, which began with *Enumeración de la patria* in 1942, her most successful prose belongs to the stories that make up the volumes *La furia* (1959) and *Las invitadas* (1961). What one finds in her prose is an attempt to transcend the trivial, routine reality enveloping the lives of most of her protagonists. She introduces symbolic creations of the characters' subconscious which all too often destroy any possible rational order.

In the title story of *Las invitadas,* the seven girls whor are invited to an adolescent boy's party represent the seven capital sins. As usual, Silvina Ocampo insists on observing her protagonists with a sharp and

25

pitiless eye, discovering fear, pride, shame, sexual hunger and frustration, sometimes tenderness, always vulnerability. In "The Prayer," from the collection *La furia,* the reader encounters the elements of self-deception, guilt, sexual urges and their repression, a need for redemption on the part of the narrator, and a desire to seek revenge for having an unfulfilled existence.

PROSE BIBLIOGRAPHY

Viaje olvidado, 1937 (stories)

Antología de la literatura fantástica (in collaboration with Jorge Luis Borges and Adolfo Bioy Casares), 1940. Augmented version, 1965, publisher Sudamericana (stories)

Autobiografía de Irene, 1948 (stories)

La furia, 1959 (stories)

Las invitadas, 1961 (stories)

Los que aman odian (in collaboration with Adolfo Bioy Casares), 1962 (novel)

The Prayer

Silvina Ocampo

Laura was in church, praying:

Lord, won't you reward the good deeds of your servant? I realize that at times I have erred. I have been impatient or have lied. I lack the spirit of charity, but I have always asked for Your forgiveness. Have I not spent hours on end kneeling on the floor in my room before the image of one of Your virgins? And that horrid boy I have hidden in my house to save him from being lynched, won't that action count in my favor? I am childless, an orphan, and I do not love my husband. You know this. I am hiding nothing from You. My parents made me get married just as they made me go to school or to the doctor. I obeyed their wishes because I thought that everything would work out all right. But love does not materialize because someone orders it, and even You could not make me love my husband without first inspiring that love in me. When he embraces me I feel like fleeing, like hiding in a forest (since early childhood I have always fantasized about an enormous forest, covered by snow, in which I can hide all my unhappiness), and he tells me:

"How cold you feel . . . like marble."

I even prefer the ugly ticketseller who sometimes gives me a pass to watch a movie with my younger sister, or the somewhat repulsive-looking shoe salesman who caresses my foot between his legs when I try on some shoes, or the blond mason at the corner of Corrientes and 9 de Julio, next to the house where my favorite pupil lives. I actually do like the mason with his blue eyes who eats bread with onion, grapes and meat sitting on the ground and who asked me: "Are you married?" and without waiting for an answer goes on to say: "What a shame."

He made me walk around the scaffolding to look at the construction of an apartment for some newlyweds.

I returned four times to this construction site. The first time it was in the morning, and the workers were cementing bricks to build an intermediate wall. I sat down on some wooden tiles. It was really a dream house! The mason (his name is Anselmo) took me up to the top to get a good view. Lord, you know that Your servant had no intention of staying very long, but I twisted my ankle and had to spend a long time amidst all those men until the pain went away. The second time I arrived in the afternoon. They were putting glass in the window frames, and I went to look for my coin purse that I always leave somewhere. Anselmo wanted me to see the terrace. It was six o'clock when we came down and all of the workers had left. Brushing against a wall I dirtied my arm and cheek with plaster. Anselmo took out a handkerchief and without permission began to clean me up. I could see that his eyes were blue and his lips very pink. I probably looked too long because he said: "Boy, what eyes you have!"

We walked hand in hand around the scaffolding. He asked me to come back at eight the next evening; one of his friends would play the concertina and the wife of another worker would bring some wine. You know, Lord, that I made the sacrifice of going there because I did not want to offend him. Anselmo's friend was playing the concertina when I arrived. Under the light of a lantern everybody gathered around the bottles of wine. The woman brought glasses and we drank. I left before the party was over. Anselmo took a flashlight and showed me the exit. He wanted to accompany me, but I did not let him.

"Are you coming back?" he said as we shook hands, "you haven't seen the tiles yet."

"What tiles?" I asked laughingly.

"The ones in the bathroom," he answered as if he were kissing me. "Come back tomorrow. They'll be here."

"Who is they?"

"The couple. We can spy on them."

"I am not used to spying."

"I'll show you the neon sign. Shoes with wings. Ever seen them?"

"Never."

"I'll show them to you tomorrow."

"All right."

"You'll come?"

"Yes," I said and left.

The next time there was nobody in the building. Behind a wooden fence burned an open fire; a few stones were holding up a pot.

"I'm the watchman for tonight," said Anselmo when I got there.
"And the couple?"
"They've left. Shall we go up and look at the neon sign?"
"All right," I answered, covering up my nervousness.

Believe me, Lord, I had no idea what was going to happen on the seventh floor. My heart was beating fast because we had walked up so many flights and I was all alone in the building with this man. When we got to the top I was glad to watch the neon sign. The shoes with wings flashed in the dark. I felt afraid. The bannister was not yet installed and I eased back into the bedroom. Anselmo put his arm around my waist.

"Don't fall now," he said, and then added: "This is where they'll put the bed. It must be nice getting married and having a love nest."

As he was talking he sat on the floor next to a little suitcase and a bundle of clothes.

"You want to see some pictures? Sit down." I sat. Lord, he opened the suitcase and took out some photos.

"This here was my mother," he said, getting closer. "See how pretty a woman she was." He began to address me in the familiar *tu* form. "And this here is my sister," he added breathing the words in my face.

He cornered me and began to put his arms around me, hardly letting me breathe. Lord, You know I tried to get away from his embrace. It was useless. I even pretended to be hurting to make him behave. You know that I left the place in tears. I am keeping nothing from You. I got home with my dress torn. In spite of this, I went back the next day because I was looking for my coin purse again. I keep nothing from You, Lord. I know that I am not a virtuous woman, but do You know very many? I am not one of those who wear tight pants and show half of their breasts when they go for a walk along the river on Sundays. My husband would not like that of course, but I could dress like that when he is not around. It is not my fault that men look at me: they see in me a sort of child-woman. It is true that I am still young, but that is not the reason they like me. They never look at Rosaura or Clara when those two walk down the street, and I bet that nobody says anything to them when they go to the beach, not even a lewd remark that is so easy to come by. I am good-looking. Is that a sin in itself? It is much worse to be embittered. Ever since I married Alberto it has been my bad luck to live on this dark street in that horrible suburb of Avellaneda. You know, Lord, that street is not even paved, and at night I twist my ankles trying to get home when wearing high heels. On rainy days I have to wear rubber boots that are torn and a rain coat that looks more like a bag. Of course, bags are in fashion now. I am a piano teacher and could have become a concert pianist if my husband and my lack of vanity had not put a stop to that. Sometimes when we have guests, he insists that I play tangos and jazz. I sit down and play, feeling humiliated and obeying him against my wishes because I know that he likes my playing. There is little joy in my life. Every day, but for Saturdays and holidays, I walk along España Street at the same hour to get to the home of one of my pupils. There is one particular section of the lonely, unpaved street with a water-filled ditch where my thoughts so often turn to You. About three weeks ago (it seems an eternity now) I saw five boys playing there. Absent-mindedly I watched them playing in the mud next to the ditch, almost as if they were not real. Two of them were fighting. One had taken away a yellow and bluish kite from the other and clutched it to his chest. The other boy grabbed him by the neck and held his head under the water in the ditch. They struggled for a while: one to keep the head under water, the other to come up for air. Bubbles appeared on the surface of the muddy water. The one boy kept the other's head submerged and the victim's strength was ebbing away. The other boys were cheering. Time can play tricks on one. I was witnessing the scene as if watching it on a movie screen, not thinking that I could have intervened. When the boy let go of the other's head the body sank into the muddy water. There was a commotion and the children fled. I now realized that I had witnessed a crime, a crime amidst children's games that seem so innocent. The children ran home shouting that Amancio Araoz had been killed by Claudio Herrera. I pulled Amancio out of the ditch. After that the women and men of the district, armed with sticks and metal pipes, wanted to lynch Claudio Herrera. Claudio's mother who liked me a lot cried and asked me to hide the boy in my house. I accepted after leaving the body to be shrouded. My house is at quite a distance from the Araoz's place, and that made things easier. At the funeral the people did not cry over Amancio, they cursed Claudio. They went around the block behind the coffin and stopped at every door shouting insults at Claudio Herrera so that people would find out what happened. They were so excited that they actually seemed to enjoy the whole thing. The white coffin was covered with attractive flowers that impressed the women. A number of children who did not even know the dead boy followed the cortège because they had nothing better to do. None cried because they were too angry. Only Miz Carmen sobbed because she did not understand what had happened. My God, that funeral really had no class at all. Claudio Herrera is eight years old. Who can tell how much he was aware of having committed a crime. I protect him like a mother. I feel happy without really knowing why. I made the little front room into a bedroom, that is where he stays. In the backyard where the chicken coop used to be I put a swing and a hammock; I also bought him a pail and a shovel to start a little garden and have fun with the plants. Claudio likes me or at least he acts as if he does. He obeys my orders better than his mother's. I told him not to let himself be seen from the balcony or the terrace and never to answer the phone. He never disobeyed me. He helps me with the dishes after dinner; he cleans and peels vegetables and sweeps the patio in the morning. I can't complain; however, maybe due to my neighbors' influence I am beginning to suspect that the boy is truly a born criminal. I am certain, Lord, that he has tried several times to kill my dog Jasmin. First I noticed that he put roach poison in his food dish; then he tried to drown him in the sink and in the bucket we use to wash the patio. I am sure that for a few days the boy gave the dog no water or he mixed it with ink; Jasmin naturally refused to drink that and started to bark. I blame Jasmin's diarrhea on some diabolical mixture he put in his meat. I went to have a talk with my doctor since she has always given me good advice. She also knows that I keep a lot of drugs in my medicine chest, including barbituates. So she told me: "Honey, lock that chest. Crime committed by children is on the increase. They will do anything to satisfy their instincts. They read dictionaries. Nothing escapes them. They know every trick. The boy could poison your husband whom he does not like according to you."

I answered her: "You have to trust human beings if you want them to turn out to be good. If Claudio suspects that I don't trust him, he would be capable of doing something terrible. I already explained to him what is in each of the bottles and showed him the ones that have a red label with the word poison written on it."

Lord, I did not lock the cabinet; I did it on purpose so that Claudio could learn to repress his criminal instincts if indeed he had them. The other night at dinnertime my husband sent the boy to the attic to get a box with carpentry tools. My husband's hobby is carpentry. When the boy failed to come down my husband went after him and found him drilling a hole in that lacquered box he loves so dearly. Upset, he beat the boy and brought him downstairs by his ear. My husband has no imagination. Since he was dealing with a child that we suspected of being abnormal, how could he punish him in a way that would have made even me mad with rage. We finished our dinner in silence. As usual, Claudio said good night. When we were alone my husband told me: "This monster will be the death of me if he does not leave this house soon."

"How can you be so impatient," I replied, "can't you see that I am doing a labor of love, Christian love?" And right there I invoked Your name.

Before going to bed we each took a sleeping pill because we both suffered from insomnia: he does not sleep and keeps me awake reading the paper or a book and lighting his cigarettes, and all along I am waiting for him to sleep. I believe that the doctor was right about locking that medicine chest. But I paid no attention to it because I insist that the best policy is to show confidence in a person. My husband disagrees. In the last few days he has become suspicious. He claims that the coffee has a strange taste and that after drinking it he feels dizzy, something that never happened to him before. To quiet him down, I lock the cabinet while he is home. Then I unlock it again. My friends no longer come to see me; I can't have them in because none of them knows my secret outside of the doctor and You who knows all. But I am not unhappy. I know that one day I shall be rewarded and that day I shall feel content again, just the way I felt when I was single and lived next to the Palermo Gardens in a little house that exists only in memory. How strange I feel today, Lord. I could spend the whole day in this church and almost could say that I have foreseen this possibility because I brought some chocolates in my purse to still my hunger. It is way after lunch time and I have not eaten anything since seven this morning. I am not a glutton, but You know that I am somewhat anemic and the chocolate will provide some energy. I don't know why I fear that something has happened at home; premonitions. Those women over there looking like harpies, with black hats and feathers, symbolize a fatal event. Has anybody ever hidden in one of your confessionals? It is really an ideal place for a child to hide. Am I not like a child right now? When the priest and these women covered with feathers leave, I shall open the door of the confessional and slip inside. I will not confess myself with a priest, only with You. I shall spend the whole night in Your company. Lord, I know that You will reward the good deeds of your faithful servant.

SILVINA BULLRICH

Silvina Bullrich was born in 1915. Her grandparents had been landed gentry whose fortunes had declined. As a child, Silvina lived in Paris; later she developed a life-long love affair with French culture and literature. Somehow she had always known that there existed an inner need to express herself as a prose writer. This need was coupled to the awareness of wanting to select certain subject matters that with few exceptions were to dominate her huge output dating from 1953 to the present. These subject matters dealt with the exploration of the conflicts, ambitions, defects and hypocracies of the Argentine upper and upper middle class and the urge to place the Argentine woman squarely into the center of this context.

No one has more played the consistent chronicler of Argentine bourgeois mores in a highly dynamic society and examined the lot of the woman during this constant transition than Silvina Bullrich. While the nameless housewife in *Bodas de cristal* (1953) is uncapable of leaving her husband, being psychologically and professionally untrained to fend for herself in an unsheltered world, Silvina Bullrich's later heroines have undergone a considerable change. The female narrator of *Mañana digo basta* (1968) is ready to stop playing the role of the passive, duty-bound mother and take full charge of her destiny, although, as the title indicates, she will do it tomorrow. But seven years later in *Te acordarás de Taormina* the author presents us with a generation clash in which the daughter tells her mother sarcastically that the Argentine woman faced the unenviable choice of contemplating prostitution or marriage.

Yet, Silvina Bullrich would hardly consider herself a rabid feminist. Side by side with the woman who is openly rebelling against patriarchy and machismo, we find many of her heroines yearning to be understood and accepted by the male as a complement, not as a rival.

Of all the popular Argentine women writers, Silvina Bullrich has proven to be the most popular one. Practically a million Argentine women identify with the needs and frustrations of the protagonist of *Mañana digo basta;* and it would be hard to find a male Argentine author who has come up with as many best sellers as Bullrich. Of the two stories selected for this anthology, "The Lover" deals with one of her favorite topics: the selfishness and sterility in the lives of the members of Argentina's upper class. "Self-denial" recreates the writer's dilemma of not knowing how to combine the need for self-assertion with the urge to live a feminine existence.

BIBLIOGRAPHY

All works are novels unless otherwise indicated

Bodas de cristal, 1953

Teléfono ocupado, 1955

Un momento muy largo, 1957

Mientras los demás viven

El hechicero, 1961

Los burgueses, 1964

Los salvadores de la patria, 1965

La creciente, 1967

Historias inmorales, 1967 (stories)

La redoma del primer ángel, 1967

El calor humano, 1970

Los monstruos sagrados, 1971

George Sand, 1972 (biography)

Mal don, 1973

Su excelencia envió el informe, 1974

Carta abierta a los hijos, 1974

Te acordarás de Taormina, 1975

Será justicia, 1976

Reunión de directorio, 1977

Los despiadados, 1978

Escándalo bancario, 1980

The Lover

Silvina Bullrich

I shall never forgive Rolo for what he did to us: he made us utterly
miserable. Now life at home is hell. And to think that we were so happy, so
easy to live with. I really do not believe that any family could have been
closer. But that was before Rolo let us down. Mother certainly did not
deserve such a fate, and neither did we. As my Aunt Sylvia said when she
saw Mother looking so wretched, certain things are just not done. I agreed
with her, of course, but I dared not say so, because I was not supposed to
be listening. There is a limit to everything. Life would be so simple if we
never had to consider others, but human beings are not like oranges to be
sucked dry and then discarded. You just cannot do that, Rolo.

After Aunt Sylvia left, I threw myself on my bed, crossed my hands
behind my head, and thought. When did it all begin? For the life of me, I
cannot remember exactly why Rolo came to our house, nor when I first
noticed that eating with us had become a habit with him. Mother, Rolo is
calling. She used to pick up the telephone, carry it into her room, and close
the door. She did not say much, but I noticed that she laughed a lot. I
wondered why. Rolo wants you to go down to meet him. He is coming for
you at nine. Rolo called. He wants you to call back. Rolo left these
flowers.

It all seemed so natural. Dad was very fond of Rolo. He used to slap
him heartily on the back when he arrived, and went out of his way to say
goodbye to him as he left. Dad, wait for me! I'm going to Clara's cocktail
party. You can drop me off since you drive past her house. Be quick then.
I'm in a hurry. Just a second. I must put on some lipstick. I can't wait.
Don't you worry. I'll take her, said Rolo. I was delighted because Dad's
car is only an ordinary sedan, whereas Rolo had a fabulous sports car that
was really out of this world.

Mother was flustered. What's going on here? She knew very well that Rolo had arrived. It's Rolo. Monica, I'm leaving now, Dad shouted out as he made for the door. But what about Nica and Patricia . . . Rolo is going to take them . . . see you later. Will you be back for dinner? No. All right.

Dad used to rush off like that, but Rolo was there. Either Nica or I used to get him a whisky and then plump down eagerly on the settee beside him. He was always full of surprises. He pointed out a parcel lying on the table. What is it? Caviar. Caviar? What a treat! . . . we've got some champagne. Do hurry up and get dressed, or we shall be late! grumbled Nica. But first I've got to open this can. Rolo is hungry. Here, give it to me. I obeyed grudgingly. I adored being with Rolo. He was far superior to our pimple-faced boyfriends; he was so intelligent, so much a man of the world, and so well-dressed. If ever I marry anyone, it will be Rolo, I said one day. Mother burst out laughing, but Nica only glared at me disapprovingly. Why on earth did you say that, she asked me later. What did I say? You know very well what you said . . . No, I don't . . . About marrying Rolo. And why not? Didn't you realize that Mother didn't like it? You're crazy. Nica hooted with laughter. You're either terribly naive or hopelessly stupid. I'm fifteen. That's right, then you're just stupid.

Nica was seventeen. She and Rolo used to talk mysteriously together for hours, stopping abruptly whenever I came in. Why are you whispering? We're not. Yes, you are. Don't be silly! One day I cornered Rolo: Why do you whisper like that with Nica? He burst out laughing: she confides in me, he said. Then he told me that Nica did not know whether or not she should encourage Juancho and that he was advising her.

So when Lalo began courting me, I went to Rolo. Wait until he graduates, he said. Lalo was only a freshman then and, after all, I was only fifteen, not like Nica who was past seventeen and anxious to get married. Besides, I was happy at home. Life was good.

I shall always remember those Sundays in November. Mother would say: Would you like to go for a trip in Rolo's launch? Would we! May I invite Lalo? Yes. And Juancho? I don't know. Ask Rolo. Perhaps it will be overcrowded. What does it matter? We can't all squeeze around that little table for lunch. A sandwich is enough for me. That's all very well, but Jorgito is coming with a friend of his.

Jorgito was Rolo's fourteen year-old son who, incidentally, turned out to be a very disagreeable specimen. Mother used to say that he was much better mannered than we were, and Nica even went so far as to agree that he would be a real "dreamboat" when he was a little older. At that time, however, he reminded me of those freckled, tow-haired dead-end kids in the North American movies.

Rolo taught us to water-ski. Lalo used to act like a two year-old, although he was over eighteen at the time. I think sometimes that he stayed with me for over a year just because of those launch trips.

Rolo, are we going out on Sunday? It's too cold. But . . . that doesn't matter does it? Please, Rolo. Sometimes he gave in. It depended largely on how Mother felt about it. She did not really enjoy those launch trips very much because she liked to have Rolo to herself, perhaps to go to the cinema and then eat in some restaurant afterwards. We promise to come back early. Mother ignored my plea. It would be far better to lunch in town and then go to a matinee because we would not have to book seats. It would be easy to get in. That's not true. When it is raining we have to stand in line. At least, we don't have to tip, Mother argued. But Rolo does the tipping. Well, it's not right, that's all, she snapped. You are always so dumb, sighed Nica afterwards. Don't you understand anything? You're as blind as a bat. You couldn't see the woods for the trees! I'm not half as dumb as you are. If I didn't keep pestering them, we would never go out in the launch. Nica just shrugged and walked away.

When we did not go out in Rolo's launch, Jorgito went off with his friends. The following Sunday, in particular, he infuriated me with his condescending manner. He took it upon himself to explain where things were kept, soda, coca-cola, everything, as if we were outsiders. Mother spoiled Jorgito terribly: she gave him whisky behind Rolo's back, and chocolates which only made him fatter than ever. I remember that Rolo used to complain that he was as plump and rounded as a woman; he even left orders at the prep school for Jorgito to be put on a strict diet. Mother always made us stand aside to allow Jorgito to water-ski first because he liked it so much. Occasionally she and Rolo went to visit him in his prep school in Quilmes. Mother used to take him hand-knitted woolens; she never knitted anything for us. Rolo tried to make up for this by bringing us perfumes given to him by a friend, a purser on a French boat, and chocolates from the Belgrano factory. Mother never ate them because she did not like candy. Juancho and Lalo were especially delighted when Rolo gave us theater tickets because their parents were very strict.

Rolo, couldn't you get us tickets for the Ballet Russe? Rolo, couldn't you . . . ? That's enough, leave Rolo alone, protested Mother. The next day Rolo would bring us what we wanted.

Mother and Rolo went out together almost every evening, but they always had dinner with us first. It was when they stayed at home to watch television that I felt happiest.

I really cannot remember just what Dad used to do at that time. He seemed to come and go like the characters in those awful plays that Uncle Felipe writes. Robots striding on and off stage for no apparent reason. Like those figurines revolving around the clock on that old square in Prague, said Rolo. Not Prague, Dijon, corrected Mother. Oh, they have those clocks with revolving figurines all over, said Rolo; but, really, your brother-in-law should take time to think up reasons for making his characters come on stage. They come on stage to drink a whisky, said Mother. That's not a very good reason! Dad has no special reasons either for coming home or going out again. He does not even need to bring money, because Mother has plenty. At any rate, he does not bother anyone, because he is always so even-tempered. He always seemed in a good mood even when Rolo made such a mess of things. Nica says that Rolo is not really to be blamed. It is that scatter-brained Fernanda's fault. She went all out to get him because he is such a good catch. I am not so sure that it is just because he is a good catch. I only know that after having known Rolo, all other men seem dull. Rolo is like a sun, a little sun, generous and always smiling. Rolo was our sun.

Didn't Rolo call today? No. Ah!

That is how it all began. Soon Mother dared not ask that question because she knew what the answer would be. It became, Did anyone call? Sylvia, Carlitos and Grandfather. No one else? No, no one else. I would have given anything to have been able to answer, Rolo called, but I could not lie.

Are you going out again tonight? Dad looked at her uneasily and surprised. After all, he had dined at the Club every single night for the past eight years. The Club, the Club, always the Club. Would he never realize that his wife was still young and attractive? She was bored, tired of always eating alone. She rushed into her bedroom crying. Dad went in after her and slammed the door. I could not hear what he said, but his voice sounded irritated, impatient. Dad stamped out of the house that night without saying a word to us. A little later, Mother rang for the maid and told her that she would eat in her room because she did not feel well. Nica and I began our dinner alone. She turned on the television, and I put on some Palito Ortega records. Mother sent word to say that we were not to make so much noise because she had a terrible headache. Nonetheless, we could hear the constant murmur of her voice as she chatted on the telephone to

Sylvia and Martha. She said some things in French though Martha understood French even less than we did, and we had been to an English prep school.

One day Rolo called. He came before dinner. He asked about Lalo and Juancho, brought us glazed chestnuts, just as if nothing had ever happened, but we were so numb with misery that we did not appreciate his jokes, nor his chestnuts. Mother said that she would rather eat out. They both left.

About three o'clock in the morning, I heard them come back. Come in, said mother. Rolo must not have moved, and neither did I, even though I ached in every limb because I was huddled up in an awkward position to listen. Come on in already; I'm not going to rape you, said mother in a voice that sounded strangely vulgar and yet pitiful. Please God, make him come in, I prayed. Make him come back to us so that we shall be as happy as we were before, and Mother will laugh again, and Dad will be in a good mood, and Mother will stay at home, and Nica and I will not be alone anymore. He did not come in. No, Monica, that would only make things worse. That's life. We have to face the facts and accept things the way they are. I remember that Dad always used to say that Rolo was not very intelligent, and that night I had my doubts: surely he could have been more gentle, more thoughtful. We can still be friends, can't we Rolo? Mother's voice was almost a moan. Later, perhaps. Why later? Why not now?

ROLO! His name shattered the silence of the night. Rolo, please, just once more, let me see you just once more, that's not asking much, only to see you. Rolo's footsteps drew nearer again. I told you that it would only make things worse, Monica. Can't you see how silly you are being? Later, when you've calmed down a little. I'm perfectly calm. Yes, I know, but why don't you get some rest now? I'll call you tomorrow. You promise? Yes. When shall I see you? ROLO! I heard the elevator door slam. ROLO! Mother rushed down the stairs. She came up again a few minutes later. I had seen Rolo's car pull off before she reached the sidewalk.

When I awoke next morning, they told me that Mother had just come back. From where? From the emergency ward. She didn't feel well last night, but she's all right now. The main thing is not to worry her, be nice to her, try to cheer her up. Dad brought home some beautiful roses and a gold bracelet. Here, take this bracelet to your mother. Tell her that I'll bring her some diamonds next time. Mother only smiled sadly. Leave it on the light table, she murmured and closed her eyes again. Dad came in timidly, went slowly up to her bed, and passed his hand over her brow. Come on now!

Where's the bravest woman in Buenos Aires? Mother only gave a wan smile and pressed his hand. You'll soon forget all this, Monica. I've been through it myself. You've just got to pull yourself together. Mother sobbed quietly. Mariano came, took her pulse, and recommended two or three days of rest. It was really lucky that Dad had acted so promptly and called him in time. Can't you take her to Europe? I'll see what I can do. But then he did nothing. They went nowhere.

Once in a while they go out together now, but when Dad says that he is off to the Club, Mother goes out alone. Oodles of people come looking for her. She spends her weekends on Martha's ranch or on Carlito's yacht. Now, when she asks, Who called?, we give her a long, confusing list of names and telephone numbers. She makes a note of them all, takes a quick bath, gets dressed, and goes out. Don't wait for me. I'm eating out.

Now Nica and I have our meals alone. She broke off with Juancho, but no one knew about it. Mother did not even notice how puffy her eyes were from crying so much. Lalo comes now and then and tries to console us, but he is so terribly childish; besides, unlike Rolo, he has no money to buy us expensive gifts, he doesn't own a car, nor does he tell funny stories. We turn on the television out of sheer boredom; and we don't need him along for just that.

Rolo should never have treated us so badly. He should have thought about us at least, even if he did not consider Mother's feelings. We tried our best to be nice to him. It would not hurt him to come and eat with us once in a while; after all, we have the best cook in Buenos Aires, the only one who still knows how to make desserts, according to Grandmother, and Dad has always bought the very best wines from the Club . . . but what is the use? Now we have neither wines nor desserts because we do not want to put on weight. With Rolo, it was so different: we did not even notice what we ate, and he always had a second helping of everything.

Rolo should never have let us down like this.

Self-Denial

Silvina Bullrich

Mother was both a romantic and old-fashioned woman. She had always been old-fashioned, even when she was fifteen; her childhood friends told me so. And I laughed about it not realizing that she was bringing me up romantic and old-fashioned too.

My life history lacks importance. I don't want to be like one of those people who meet a real writer and never stop pestering him with the story of their lives because they believe it will make for a most interesting book. The reason is obvious: I realized that self-explanatory events are not enough to make up a book; and if someone should write it, the result would be a dismal failure.

I got married, got divorced, had a lover, another one, a third. The first one left me; I ditched the second one because I met somebody else. With the next one it ended in a draw. There isn't much point in dwelling on the subject. Then there were a few casual encounters, really not as sordid as some novelists make them out to be; it was all in fun and sometimes we parted as good friends and other times we didn't. But to tell the truth, friendship has nothing to do with a one-night stand.

I'm actually fairly smart. I work for Aerolineas Argentinas, and my co-workers will testify that I am very efficient. That's actually my curse: to be very efficient. My poor romantic and old-fashioned mother drilled it into my head during the first twenty years of my life—and forever after—that the most important things in life are to be efficient, responsible and unselfish. Her advice worked like the famous Chinese water torture that may have been a myth, but nevertheless made such an impression on the Western mind: her advice drilled a hole into my head, penetrated my brain, touched my heart and slid down to my sex organ. And so my brain, my heart, my sex organ turned out to be selfless, efficient, reticent but

43

generous, filled with a certain dignity, moral purpose and purity. But let's be frank here for a minute, I knew what I as doing. I assimilated my mother's preachings but, in the process, modified them a little. Thus it never crossed my mind that I would go straight to hell for having gone to bed with Luis, just as I doubted very much that the general manager's secretary had her place waiting for her in heaven because at the age of forty-three she was still a virgin who refused to shave her legs and considered the use of contact lenses to be a cardinal sin. I also doubt very much that Hitler and I are destined to suffer similar punishment in another world. That would be presumptious of me.

But I might as well confess it now: I believed seriously that nothing ties a man more to a woman (even if she is not his wife) than the awareness that she does not bother him with her problems, dries her tears before he arrives, covers up her daily disappointments, remakes her old dress instead of asking for a new one, pretends to despise oversized cars because they are too showy and hard to park, thinks that in this moderate climate no one needs a fur coat, that fine jewelry is a nuisance and that imitations are just as good, that nowadays you can eat better in a cheap restaurant, that maid service is unnecessary and even spoils intimacy, that the modern woman can take care of herself as well as a man can, and that, in the final instance, the poor are less unhappy than the rich because nobody has bothered to bring out a handbook about the conditions of the wealthy.

Men are more intelligent than women, but not in the way they think they are. Good God, all you have to do is listen to political candidates the night before the elections in order to get a true idea of men's mental capacity; and I could go on from there if I wanted to. Men are more intelligent than women in the game of love. Cheating for countless generations in business and wars taught them an infallible tactic: to convince the opponent that he had some remarkable qualities which in reality benefitted the challenger. Luis benefitted from the fact that I worked, knew how to cook and believed in the manual of feminine frugality that I had mentioned earlier.

"If you don't mind, let's eat any old thing in your place or mine. I've worked all day and am too tired to go out to eat."

I had worked all day too but refrained from reminding him. It would have been a lack of tact, femininity and affection, and besides he would have used it to get back at me during our next quarrel. So I just fidgeted.

"Don't bother, fix anything, boil a couple of eggs."

But I knew he liked French omelettes and opened a can of

mushrooms, and since there was milk I could fix a rice dessert in two minutes; or, if he agreed, I could make a spaghetti à la Parisienne with left-over chicken and cream. I set the table, toasted the bread, brewed some strong coffee. It's really nothing, all will be ready in a jiffy, have another whisky while you wait, no, don't bother buying a bottle, I can get one more easily than you . . . no, silly, our pilots don't do any smuggling, but some passengers get generous because we let them through with excess luggage or an expired passport . . . just a couple of minutes more . . .

And so everything would be ready, if not in ten minutes, at the most in half an hour. And I kept on going, putting rollers in my hair when I could hardly stand up straight, redoing my make-up, swooning over his male ardor when he produced it, or proclaiming that it was lucky that he felt so tired because tonight I couldn't have done it even with Alain Delon. He liked the "sporty" look in women's clothes, which really meant last year's fashions; and so I told him that I had neither time nor interest in getting myself a new outfit and that there were more important things to consider doing in life although he never asked me what they were. We met almost daily just as we would have met the waiter at the local pizzeria if we had been eating there. We were not unhappy, really, but at the same time neither one of us was waiting for the happy ending to flash across the screen.

One of my girl friends told me one day that my method was all wrong. What method? Playing the selfless female, she said, because a man never sticks to a woman like that, he always sticks to his investment. I did not understand that at all, and so she explained it to me presenting undisputable evidence. A demanding woman is the most successful one because even a rich man cannot afford a new apartment, a new car or a new fur coat every time he falls in love; and so he will think an awfully long time before breaking with a woman that represents a considerable capital investment for him. Her reasoning seemed pretty logical to me and I promised to think about her advice, but it was already too late. Luis was not about to invest an ice cream cone in me any more.

About that time he told me that Julita was the most charming woman that ever walked the earth. She's like a little bird, a humming bird, she goes through life without being touched by its ugliness; and we were to pick her up to go to the movies. And why can't she come over here since she has a car and we don't? Come here all by herself at eight o'clock in the evening? She hates being out alone at night and we can easily walk to her place. We went. On the way back we left her at her place and walked home nine blocks in the drizzle. She could have dropped us off, I said. Open the garage door all by herself at night? Luis was really upset. Between the two they had worn me to a frazzle. Julita had shown up dressed to kill, in a halo of perfume and all smiles. You look divine, said Luis. Doesn't she look divine? Yes, I said. Had she had dinner? She hadn't. That's alright, said Luis, we'll have a cup of coffee while you grab a bite, and if it gets to be too late, we'll go to the second show. We went to the second show because Julita didn't grab a "bite," but polished off a full dinner. After taking in a movie I am usually thirsty, but I kept my mouth shut. I didn't even have a coin for the toilette. Have a heart, Luis, and buy some flowers from that poor woman who is standing out here in the cold, said Julita. How right you are, we are all so selfish nowadays, said Luis, including me as if he did not know that I never asked him for anything in order to save him money. I looked at my watch. I start my job at nine in the morning, I ventured timidly. How horrible to have to work, sighed Julita; I guess I am old-fashioned but I believe that a woman ought not to work, it makes her less feminine. Then how does she manage to make a living? If a woman is not capable of having a man look after her she isn't a real woman, Julita said seriously; then she broke out in a smile: I am really so useless, I can't even write a check; at the bank the male tellers laugh and do it for me. Please come to me when you need anything done, Luis was begging. All I need is money in my account because banks have the bad habit of returning checks with insufficient funds. How inconsiderate of them, laughed Luis who by now was absolutely ecstatic. While Julita kept up her scatterbrain girlish act Luis was in seventh heaven.

By now I had gotten the message. Not that I minded it so much, because I knew all along that some day this thing between us had to come to an end, and I actually am not sure that it had ever gotten off the ground. To tell the truth, it was the best way out. I had been castrating Luis, and Julita obviously would make a full man out of him. It was perhaps masochism or sadism or simply curiosity that kept me from offering Luis his freedom right there and then. I got a certain kick out of watching these two.

I have to take care of Julita's taxes. Have to rush to see Julita: she's been at the dentist's and drilling drives her up the wall. Poor girl, brought up in luxury, so well bred, and now with money troubles. Julita can't stand the cold weather, Julita can't stand the heat either, Julita can't cook . . . she has other talents.

And Luis was running around in circles looking for solutions to

Julita's problems. Her whole life seemed to consist of a series of problems: the dentist's drilling, the maid who quit, the china that broke, the car that stopped running, her mother's operation although they never operated on her. Then there were the personal, intimate problems that would lie beyond the comprehension of somebody as practical and insensitive as myself: the problem of not being able to communicate, depression, emptiness, loneliness, guilt complexes, superiority complexes, inferiority complexes, she had them all. Luis naturally made the round to the psychiatrists with her, he took her away from Buenos Aires for the winter because the cold was bad for her, and also for the summer because she could not stand the heat nor sleep with an air conditioner whirring; he finally put her up in a cozy hotel because she was too tired to fight with the servants that nowadays steal you blind or quit without even giving notice.

Then, one day, they just dropped out of sight. Once I saw her walking down the street very elegantly dressed with a pearl-grey poodle on the leash. Then I met Pedro. I might have fallen for him and he might have gone for me. But I also felt a tremendous weariness bearing down on me. I knew that I no longer had the energy to fix the little dinners that would make me look like the total woman, nor could I have mustered the emotion to sigh deeply in front of every flower girl standing out there in the cold or get upset over any of the little problems that each day brings.

Sometimes when I feel a surge of my poor, misled mother's romantic blood in my veins, I daydream about a special man who'd come into my life: he'd see me laughing and ask me why I was crying and kiss away the tears that I did not shed; he'd see me trying to take on the whole world and quietly ask me why I am trembling so; when I'd rush off on a trip, he'd ask me why I was running away; and looking at my attempts at being worldly, stubborn and aggressive, he'd exclaim sadly: "I never knew that a woman could be so weak."

MARIA ANGELICA BOSCO

Maria Angelica Bosco was born in Buenos Aires in 1917 and has been active as an essayist, translator and fiction writer. Her Spanish translation of Flaubert's *Madame Bovary* earned her wide acclaim. As a fiction writer, she has cultivated the detective novel and written film scripts in that genre. On the other hand, her "serious" novels explore the dilemma of the Argentine woman who suffers equally in marriage and divorce due to a lack of self-fulfillment. In her novel *Donde está el cordero?* (1965), the author unfolds the meaningless life of a woman who dares to leave the "Doll's House." Cecilia, the protagonist, comes home tired from work to an empty apartment, fearful of spending another night alone while waiting for an understanding lover who does not materialize. Living in a vacuum and without an apparent purpose, Cecilia makes the reader wonder if a man is necessary to give a woman like her the needed center of gravity since she cannot find a *raison d'être* on her own.

In her novel *La Negra Velez y su ángel* (1969), the author plunges into a feminist attack against the subservient role endured by the Argentine married woman. After seven years of marriage, the protagonist is tired of her husband's infidelities and the family's efforts to maintain proper appearances in order to assure the approval of a hypocritical bourgeois society. La Negra's rebellion collapses as she lets herself be dominated by her husband and later by her lover, both of whom expect her to obey the rules of the game. Her attempted suicide indicates the need for self-destruction due to self-betrayal.

49

Her more recent book, *Cartas de mujeres* (1975), features a number of imaginary letters written by legendary women such as Eve, Hera, and Emma Bovary. The final, and by far the longest letter, is from Maria Angélica Bosco to Esther Vilar, the German born essayist who wrote a controversial book that appeared in the United States as *The Manipulated Man.* Vilar exposes the female as a shrewd exploiter of man-the-provider, a presentation that received a devastating treatment from Bosco. The exchange of letters between Tolstoy's Anna Karenina and Ibsen's Nora, included in this anthology, go beyond the confines of the two novels and their socio-historical context, delving into the problem of the woman who feels forced to leave her family in order to follow her own dictates.

BIBLIOGRAPHY

La muerte baja en el ascensor, 1954 (detective novel)
La muerte soborna a Pandora, 1956 (detective novel)
La trampa, 1960 (novel)
El comedor de diario, 1963 (novel)
La Negra Vélez y su ángel, 1969 (novel)
Carta abierta a Judas, 1971 (novel)
Historia privada, 1972 (novel)
Cartas de mujeres, 1975 (stories and essays)
Retorno a 'La Ilusión', 1976 (essays)
En la estela de un secuestro, 1977 (detective novel)
Muerte en la costa del río, 1979 (detective novel)

Letter From Ana Karenina To Nora

Maria Angélica Bosco

Madame:

Allow me to make you a gift of a letter of protest. I feel entitled to this action because both you and I are women produced by the literature of the Nineteenth Century (which continues to influence the Twentieth Century, a period similar in many ways to one in which the barbarians menaced the Roman Empire).

You, Nora, show the world the image of a strong woman, one who pulls herself up by her bootstraps, as Simone de Beauvoir might put it. You leave your home, your husband and your children in search of your own self (your soul, as a true Russian would say) when you realize that up to that moment you had been treated like an object. In the final instance I do the same, only I leave Mr. Karenin holding on to a lover with one hand and an illegitimate child with the other one . . . But, although there are similarities in our flight from the sanctuary of marital life, there also exist many nuances that create irreconcilable discrepancies. At first glance, the defenders of romanticism who never seem to die out, might look with favor upon me; but once the passion crumbles into little pieces—something that happens very frequently—you come out the winner. Few people are given the privilege to remain more than a little while in the garden of love.

Besides, I was destined to fail, and even the Scriptures tell us: "The winner shall dress in white." My clothes show the colors of defeat and death.

And yet, you, the elegant middle-class housewife from Norway, married to a prosaic businessman, and I, an aristocratic lady, wife of a high official at the czarist Court, have a lot in common. We both share an impeccable upbringing in a bourgeois home. We both married men who impressed us with their social position and apparent prestige. We both

51

lived a very sheltered and pampered existence, unable to recognize physical and moral defects around us (I never noticed Karenin's ugly ears until I met Vronsky), we passionately adored our children, and we enjoyed social respectability as well as a constant homage to our respective beauty, feeling safe and sound within the so-called bosom of good society. It does make one feel good to appear in public harvesting approval for one's physical as well as moral beauty.

But now we come to the parting point. You were more fortunate than I. You, as a fictional character, are the daughter of a Nordic writer who came out in favor of social progress and equality for women, while I was created by a tortured Russian who never knew whether to turn left or right, someone who spent his whole life dominated—within his private hell—by the fear of sin as he tried to find God—not an easy task—through his guilt-ridden mysticism.

Just pay attention to what he does with me, the daughter of his troubled conscience. He takes me unawares and confronts me with this man Vronsky, a sort of Nineteenth-Century playboy; but since such a type did not really exist in those days, he was but a spoiled young gentleman, and to top it all off, a military man, rich and good-looking. All this makes him the fatal combination for a woman who for some reason believed that she had the right to enjoy the absolute in love. It is true the he left the service to be near me, but we both know that by displaying sincere regrets they would have handed him back his uniform. Since his manners were genteel and monetary fortune in the Russia of the czars and the serfs meant stability for the landed gentry, Vronsky held all the cards needed for social rehabilitation. On the other hand, I missed out permanently on this rehabilitation the moment I left my house without first having taken the precaution of getting a divorce, as my shrewd brother and my dear friend and relative, Betsy—who proved to be much smarter in the handling of extramarital affairs than I—had advised me to do.

Why did Tolstoy not endow me at least with the virtue of serenely accepting the inevitable? No, he fills me with despair and jealousy once the magic of my honeymoon with Vronsky has worn off. He throws me into a purgatory that comes close to being hell itself. Following our return to Moscow (after the unfortunate experience of spending two weeks in St. Petersburg we realized that that place was off-limits to us), our living together was getting more difficult day by day. In a certain way and, in spite of obstacles, Vronsky renews his ties with his mother and brother while I can do nothing to recover my son who little by little becomes a painful memory as my hopes fade away.

To sum it all up, Tolstoy slowly takes me by the hand and inexorably leads me to the railway platform and gives me the push that makes me end up under the wheels of the train. He really left the reader with a fine impression of me: a jealous and suicidal adulteress.

And to think that they are still singing Tolstoy's praises! They keep insisting that nobody but he understood the depth and despair of a passionate woman or the heroics and pitfalls of love (to be acted out by the female, of course). They pretend that his comprehension of the gamut of emotions of the feminine soul, like mine, seems to have come to him by the way of a supernatural literary talent. They ponder about the loving compassion with which he created me. Even nowadays, a whole century later, not a single reader would dare to venture that Tolstoy did not love me, reasoning that an author like him knows that he must show his love for his heroine, because otherwise he could not get the public to love her in turn. But I do grant him one thing: Tolstoy (in my opinion an omnipotent creator and objective judge who decrees the fatal outcome that would have occurred to me also in real life) endows me at least with the precious gift of spontaneity.

Like you, Nora, I have an impulsive nature. I love my son without considering society's duties or obligations. I love Vronsky before and after committing the unforgivable deed of fleeing my home. I spontaneously hate my husband, Aleksei Karenin, and pay dearly for this sentiment because it is always dangerous to mix hatred and compassion. In fact, instead of looking after my interests while there is still time and obtaining a divorce that would have assured me my son and some respect from society, I let go of everything and leave Karenin with the option of revenge, so easy to come by under the cover of duty and morality.

You see, Nora, by giving me a spontaneous nature, Tolstoy has assured me of the world's commiseration. This is my only triumph, but it will be mine forever.

It is quite easy to feel compassion, especially when dealing with a dead person. Pity then is like a coin that we leave in the hand of a beggar as we turn our back to his misery.

It could be that because of his mystical sense of all-encompassing guilt, Tolstoy made me live and die to serve as an example. If that is the case, there remains nothing for me to add. I shall serve as a warning example then. Any other woman who would dare emulate me within a similar social context would need to have an exceptional lover or an extremely boring husband. And if she decides to go ahead with it, she will either have to ignore my fate or be swept away by her passion.

Well, if that is how things stand, I will have to keep quiet. But let nobody try and tell me that this morose Russian could not have tried to give love and me a better destiny. Believe me, Nora, I would have preferred to sit on some terrace in the early evening, watching my children play and seeing the stars brighten up over the Moscovite countryside while I would repeat to myself:

"Love lasts such a short time, and oblivion is forever."

I wish that it could have been this way because I was not even given the chance to forget.

Ana

Letter From Nora To Ana Karenina

María Angélica Bosco

Madame:

I have read your letter with respect and attention. Please forgive the redundancy because attention is surely one aspect of respect. I don't want to sound pedantic, but I was created by a man obviously in love with words, and such an affliction must be borne with courage, otherwise it overwhelms us.

Mrs. Karenina (please believe that I am sorry I cannot call you Mrs. Vronsky, in keeping with my Nordic spirit): Have you ever considered what it means to close the door of your house on one of those Scandinavian afternoons or evenings, foggy and cold, to face yourself all alone? I don't mean to imply that it is less foggy or cold in Russia nor that its nights are any shorter. I certainly don't want to make any meteorological errors here. I only want to remind you that it is not the same to abandon one's home all alone as it is to do it holding on to the protective arm of a lover. Don't take these words as a reproach, dear Ana. Speaking for myself and probably any other woman in my circumstances, I confess that I would have loved to leave my home shedding tears on the lapels of a man's coat and to suppress the anguish of my lowered social status by indulging in the pleasures of love during the following night.

But I never enjoyed such a relief, and since I did not have it at my disposal, I learned to be a woman, the age-old aspiration of the female species. I learned to be a woman through my solitude and the misfortune of not being able to blame anyone for my state.

Madame Karenina, you should not go on blaming your spiritual father and creator, holding him responsible for your misfortune. The only thing you are both guilty of is not having read the Bible more carefully. In the *Book of Books* it is written that during the destruction of Sodom and

Gomorrah, Lot's wife was turned into a statue of salt for looking backwards. Madame, when one decides on a drastic change of life one must first create it in one's soul, ready to leave behind a social world that is going to be lost for good.

What I hold against you is the display of an incurable illness, one that is as old as mankind. Many people pretend to change the course of their existence but, alas, only by expecting the applause of those whom they leave behind.

And that, my dear lady, is nothing but a historical bit of nonsense. Do you know what lies behind it? Simply fear! The fear of being left alone in a wide and alien world. Only by losing our fear of loneliness will the world be ready to accommodate our need for some happiness and then it won't seem so alien anymore. We only fail when we try so hard to obtain the approval of others in order to approve of ourselves: "I don't care what others might say as long as I am doing what I want to do." And when we reach that point, the big, wide world no longer frightens us, but rather becomes an entertaining spectacle that we look at as if we were watching life from the window of a fast-moving train.

I was proven right by that episode of yours in the theater, just one of many such happenings. Why did you insist on appearing at the first-night performance of the St. Petersburg Opera? To use your beauty as a passport to social acceptance? Dear God, beauty is the oldest weapon in feminine history. Did you really expect society to approve of you as the happy adulteress? Good grief, people have a hard enough time forgiving happiness in others, much less one based on an illicit relationship. You can't impose that kind of happiness, dear Ana, you can at best live with it, modestly, unassumingly, so that it does not bother others too much.

In the Opera you experience being rejected by your society. You richly deserved that for being so obtuse. You don't cross the street against a red light without some danger of being run over. For every act there is a green and a red semaphore.

Stop complaining then about the destiny that your creator has imposed upon you. Accept the lesson that he gave you because your disastrous end was the consequence of being too spontaneous and not logical enough. Madame Karenina, you are but a minor martyr. I admit to the drawbacks of such of fate, but you ought not to complain too much. The world is filled with martyrs who had no intention of being one: slaves, soldiers, the sick, the helpless, the downtrodden, unloved children, lonely old people. You are not among these. No matter how one looks at you, you chose your own fate.

And that is better than nothing. You can complain about your lack of common sense if you wish, but just remember that there is a price to be paid for that deficiency. In our present society this price is going up rapidly; there is a sort of open season on anybody who dares to see things differently from the majority. Of course, you could not know that because you never lived in a struggling democracy.

Anyhow, it is obvious that you are not satisfied with your fate, the paradise of fulfilled love is not enough for you. Let me assure you that I have often dreamed about such a paradise. At times I have wished that my sullen creator, so preoccupied with woman's condition, had written down the second part of my life's story, putting me in some dreary boarding house where I would be awaiting the nocturnal visit of a lover, while my mind would stop looking for rational ontological explanations and my body would be anticipating love's great ritual to the point of electrifying every inch of my skin. But I was modelled after Minerva, and there is nothing I can do about it.

You and I are condemned to suffer in the eternal purgatory reserved for fictional characters that are praised or condemned by posterity according to the latest literary fashion. But when you, conscious of this situation, act indignantly because your story does not produce as many tears as you have shed during those months in which your happiness crumbled into dust, remember that an existence based on logic and common sense can make us cry just as much. Our sobs may be quieter, but hardly less painful.

Remember that to become a woman who has common sense and is ready to face adversity can mean to spend sleepless nights and tortured days. It can mean that one is slowly tearing an illusion to shreds, giving up all ambitions but one: namely to remain truthful to the woman in us that searches for a meaning in life with all her strength, her mind and sex, her fears and sorrows.

If such a vision should become reality, then destiny has been indeed very kind to her, and she can look down on life from the ramparts of her newly conquered tower. But to climb all those steps is so arduous! It is so incredibly hard to learn to control one's breathing moving from one step to the next.

Cesar Frank, the poet, left us two admirable lines that I take the liberty of quoting to provide an appropriate end to this letter, together with my esteem for our common destiny, reserved for women who have been fated to become a prototype.

There is nothing left of myself nor of him.
I am but the icy abode where passion once reigned.

Nora

SYRIA POLETTI

Born in Northern Italy in 1919, Syria Poletti later followed in the footsteps of millions of her compatriots looking for a more promising life in Argentina. But she was hardly a typical immigrant. Brushing aside the physical and moral debris left by the Second World War in her native land, Syria Poletti set out to earn a degree in Italian and Spanish literature at the Argentine University of Córdoba and then proceeded to settle in Buenos Aires where she began to earn a living as a translator, and soon participated in the world of journalism and belles lettres.

Her first book and only novel to date was *Gente conmigo,* published in 1961. In it she writes a veiled self-portrait of an Italian translator whose search for happiness is thwarted by the egotism and indifference of a number of people surrounding her and who fail to recognize her deepseated need for love and compassion. While *Gente conmigo* serves as a testimony of the author's confrontation with the New World and the uniqueness of urban Argentine culture, her later works of fiction reflect earlier preoccupations based on impressions stemming from a childhood and adolescence spent in the provincial environment of an Italy dominated by fascism, catholic traditionalism and a small-town way of life that coalesced to create a somber experience in the mind of the writer.

Syria Poletti also has written a number of children's books, and *Gente conmigo* has since been adapted to the screen. She seems to be at her best when employing a confessional mode in her writing; it lends drama as well as feeling of genuine concern for humanity to her stories even though they may be allegorical cloth. "The Final Sin," from *Linea de fuego,* is such a piece of writing, combining obvious feminine desires with the need to create universal values. Thus, her passion for life is explained through the genuine search for beauty and, in the final instance, humanity.

BIBLIOGRAPHY

Gente conmigo, 1961 (novel)
Línea de fuego, 1964 (stories)
Historias en rojo, 1967 (stories)
Extraño oficio, 1971 (essays and stories)
Taller de imaginería, 1977 (essays and stories)

The Final Sin

Syria Poletti

For him the essential element in life amounted to showing one's talent: to be a real poet. For me the ultimate thing was to love. But we could identify with each other's goals because we shared an intense passion that found its expression in an urgency to fulfill ourselves while waiting in frustration and with an undying hope to accomplish something of value.

Suddenly one day he experienced a great world-weariness and left. He killed himself. It must have been a day on which the waves of hope no longer reached up to his heart and he let the bullet out of its chamber, the bullet he had meditated about secretly, being the eternal masochist, when everything seemed to be out of joint and he needed to get even with life's nausea. It was but an absurd gesture directed at an even more absurd reality.

That was not my way. I wrote knowing that I had little or no talent, maybe because for a woman the waves of hope reach a higher water level, especially during the amorous hour. Or because the passionate hours manage to submerge everything, and one realizes that this so-called talent has really nothing to do with the primordial needs of one's being. Talent is but a pure accident in the human existence, and at times an embarrassing one.

He used to say: "We have to write something new, something worthwhile. Or nothing." And since his thoughts were lucid and deep, he found nothing new, nothing worthwhile to write about. Cornered by the implacable awareness that he needed to repudiate whatever he had written, he pulled the trigger. For him this final act constituted the only language that could be used to express the terrible tension that enveloped his rebellious spirit: to vomit his nausea.

I, however, kept on trying. I insisted in spite of myself. And now the five hundred copies of my first book had arrived by mail. A novel, of course. All women who are prone to commit suicide suffer inevitably from the illness of wanting to write a novel. And since they do not kill themselves, sooner or later they wind up writing one. That is sort of a cowardly way out, or else a naive attempt to relive old daydreams. Or maybe just inventing them. Anyhow, it seems to be a simple matter of readjusting the feminine equilibrium, no more and no less.

Be that as it may, I have spent the last fifteen years imagining the day my novel would come out with the same excitement that lived in me at the age of fifteen when I dreamed about love. I confess that I still keep the notebook in which I wrote down the possible dedications for my friends and enemies, especially my enemies. But there are not too many of them around and, besides, they would be left untouched by my book. Maybe even worse: they might begin to feel sorry for me.

But at least the novel is not officially dedicated to anybody. All those years when I was dreaming about publishing the book I constantly changed the name of the person to whom it would be dedicated. "To the long-awaited companion"; "to the man who brought meaning to my life"; "to the man who romped through my life like a savage colt destroying everything." After the first attacks of exhilaration and disillusionments I began to dream up more reasonable phrases like "to the father of my children." Finally I dedicated the book to no one because all the men in my life had disappeared.

I also shuffled the names of my friends around; but I discarded them one by one because they always disappointed me or, rather, they managed to surprise me with an unforeseen indifference.

The only thing I rejected from the beginning was to dedicate the book to a patron of the arts so that he or she would pick up the tab for the costs of the edition. Whether good, bad or indifferent, a book belongs to the writer just as much as his or her life blood. One could conceivably hand it over to a lover or a perfect scoundrel but never to a patron, and even more so when this book happens to represent an unabashed confession. The truth is that by now a number of years have gone by and the book carries the inscription "Author's Edition," a reminder that it is nothing but the result of a useless sacrifice and an obsessive willpower; and I surely would not have the vaguest idea to whom to dedicate it at this late a date. Leafing through its pages I now find them to be so repetitious, sentimental, sad in tone and autobiographic in content that I could scream. Why could I not have dissolved the overbearing truth and its subsequent bad taste by injecting some fantasy and fiction into the novel? All the book does is to project the past, present and future through the darkest of glasses, denying any possibility of new love or a rebirth of life.

I am no longer interested in sending the book to anyone. My friends from earlier days with whom I used to get together and curse the opportunists who followed the literary fashions and found a publisher will have forgotten me. They have become well placed personages, level-headed organization men, completely cured of their former intellectual escapades. My book would only make them break out in a smile, maybe mixed with an inkling of nostalgia, but certainly also a lot of complacency. Besides, they would most certainly think that using a vanity press at the age of fifty was but a consequence of a harmless mania.

Well, I might have a few friends left, but I am sure that they expected something far better from me: something overpowering perhaps. In the first place, they never imagined that I would forsake my integrity and use a vanity press. Besides, they expected a totally different kind of novel: more sensational, revealing and eccentric. The lack of erotic confessions must have deeply disappointed them. Everybody clamors for a novel that reveals disconcerting things, uncovers essential secrets and comes to a logical denouement. As if human existence were not incongruous and illogical enough already! Don't they know that for a woman to be writing means to clamor for something that is deeply rooted within her, to quell the obsessive and absurd yearning for love that rushes through her veins, or to elude the echo of a soft lullaby that bursts from her total being? My friends remember my caustic wit and expect to find pages filled with sharp, candescent images. Oversimplifications! Being caustic equals having a red-hot iron stirring the very fibers of one's being. Especially if one is a woman because a lucid state of mind does not save her from a feeling of desolation and uncertainty as she moves on her perilous journey towards a certain abyss.

If my novel should prove to be successful, my friends are going to find out about it. Then they will proclaim that they have always been my friends and believed in my talent. Then they'll say that the novel shows great promise. People always seem to say that somebody or something looks promising when they want to get around a situation that bothers them. And for a short time they'll make over me, and I'll be in fashion for a few days or even a season. And after a TV interview on a women's show or a banquet in my honor I'll return alone to my apartment, like a blown-out candle, because not a single man will have said the things to me that he would have told a twenty-year old girl walking down the street with a short story in her hand. Success promotes male desire all right, but when a woman advances in age she declines on all fronts in spite of her other triumphs.

Other friends won't even find out about the book, and that is to the good. To hide a failure has become a necessity for survival; that much I have learned over the last few years. Before I used to confess my failures and say: "I've lost such and such." But then people thought that I had lost everything and was worth nothing. Nowadays I hide my failures like a forbidden vice; the bad thing about it is, however, that failure is gnawing at my insides much stronger than any vice could have managed. And people will think anyway that I am trying to hide some unspeakable evil from them. Therefore I really prefer that nobody read the novel into which I have poured up to the last drop of my life blood, remaining empty and exhausted. Neither my life nor my book possess any real meaning; my nights keep on being as solitary as ever.

Now I find myself wrapping up my novel and taking it to the cemetery: to the name and number that correspond to a friend who committed suicide twenty years ago. Through this little present I want to make him realize that I kept on trying, walking the swaying tightrope, stubborn as a mule, as only a woman can be. He, the eternal sceptic, would just smile and say: 'You made a bad mistake! Life is nauseating, everywhere, but especially in this country. Writing or shouting about it does not change anything.'

And he would glance through the book with a lax gesture, raising his eyebrows, and suddenly start thinking about his gun as if somebody had given him a secret signal. He can't tell me otherwise. I know him. Only the gun really does not matter anymore.

And then, as if to justify my basic naiveté once again, I would reply: 'Okay, Mario, but . . . I wanted to live! I did not feel like shooting myself. I needed to wait. I wanted to find out for myself if life was as miserable and purposeless as you proclaimed it to be. And I thought that just maybe love could work its miracle. Or something like that. I assure you that while I loved I forgot all about writing, about anguish, about all those metaphysical problems that you made me talk about, and to which I returned once my lovers left me. To think—which means to suffer—seemed to be the result of the poison that you injected me with before your final take-off. Yes, I have lived. And I kept on hoping that I would live again. That is why I started to write. Believe me. I would even gladly feel again the deep disgust arising from a new encounter with men at their basest and dirtiest because in some absurd fashion a new hope would start to flow through my veins once more. I would ride the crest of that wave feeling that it is a woman's lot to want to love and produce life, and writing is nothing but a reflection of that condition. And now that my life blood has stopped stirring and love's beat has stopped, I wrote this book, published it and now feel free because I needed to commit this final sin. And through this sinful act my blood has become rejuvenated and the warmth has returned to my body. You and I know that our only vice was fashioned by those absurd dreams that you disposed of with a bullet . . . and that I continued to face by continuing to live.'

BEATRIZ GUIDO

Beatriz Guido was born in Rosario, one of Argentina's largest cities. She later studied literature in Rome and philosophy with the existentialist Gabriel Marcel in Paris. Married to Latin America's most prestigious film director, Leopoldo Torre Nilsson, who died in 1979, she became deeply involved in film making herself. She has turned a number of her novels and short stories into screenplays that were filmed by her husband and won national as well as international prizes.

Some of the recurrent themes in her writings involve the adolescent fascination with the forbidden world of sex and irrationality, the decadence of a social ruling class that is paralyzed by a worn-out philosophy of life, and the dual nature of sex leading to liberation or punishment for the woman. Beatriz Guido has always taken great care to explore the possibilities of experimenting with perceptions of reality and to discover a language that would correspond to these perceptions.

Yet, Argentina's social and political turbulence has at times prompted her to face her country's harsh realities in her prose. Thus, her novel *El incendio y las visperas* reflects Argentina under the shadow of Juan and Evita Perón, and a number of her stories portray the clash between urban terrorism and military dictatorship.

Of the two stories included here, "Ten Times Around the Block" basically underlines the duality of female and male urges in an ambiance filled with alienation, sordid sex and personal humiliation, mitigated by a contrapuntal hope for spiritual salvation. The author really comes into her

67

68

own when she is able to blend fantasy and reality in a story such as "Takeover," where the archetypal sway of the eternal femininity triumphs inexorably over the hesitant will of the male protagonist, obliterating social barriers and patriarchal mores.

BIBLIOGRAPHY

La casa del ángel, 1954 (novel)
La caída, 1956 (novel)
Fin de fiesta, 1958 (novel)
La mano en la trampa, 1961 (stories)
El incendio y las vísperas, 1964 (novel)
Escándalos y soledades, 1970 (novel)
Piedra libre, 1976 (stories)

Ten Times Around The Block

Beatriz Guido

"Where to now?" asked Laura after a long silence.

"Now it's a matter of getting a taxi, and at this hour that's almost impossible right downtown. We'd better take the subway to the Once railroad station."

"Why does it have to be precisely today, why today?"

"Well, you've got to start some time, don't you think? These meetings in tea rooms and such, they don't lead to anything. All we do is talk. Besides, I imagine it's not your first time."

"Oh no, definitely not," she answered leaning a little on his arm.

They took the subway to Once while he kept repeating himself.

"It's better to get away from downtown; at this hour nobody can find a taxi; and I don't want you to have to walk there, not even one block, do you see?"

Laura felt somehow grateful thinking that he had just mustered all the feelings he was capable of, feelings of tenderness for her, at least for this afternoon. While he was holding on to the swinging leather strap in the subway car she briefly brushed her hand against his cheek.

Finally they emerged at the big square at Once.

"We'd better walk to the next corner where there's a taxi stand, even if we have to stand in line for half an hour. How late can you get back to your boarding house?"

"Nine o'clock."

"Well, we'd better look into that business. We could meet earlier than today."

"Does it *have* to be today?" she asked again. "Why today? We could go to a movie."

69

"Come on, just follow me," he ordered with a sour tone in his voice.

Laura walked behind him taking short steps, unsure of herself, desperately hoping that somehow all the taxis in the world would disappear.

"Finally," he cried out.

"An ancient relic, a 1930 Ford convertible with celluloid curtains stopped next to them. The driver seemed jovial.

"Where to? Can I take you all the way to heaven? Careful there getting in and watch out for those straps, young lady."

Pablo leaned over towards the driver and ordered: "Hotel Azul."

"Are you sure that is the right name? The one on Pueyrredon Street?"

"Of course, I'm sure. Do you think I don't know what I'm talking about?"

"Well, it is such a beautiful afternoon," replied the driver, "why waste it in such a dark place. It's like going to vote behind a closed curtain."

Pablo became impatient. "Why don't you watch where you're going. You should have turned into Ayacucho Street."

"You'll have to excuse me, but I have to stop at my home first; it is close by and will only take a couple of minutes. Now, if you don't want to wait, that's all right with me too. Is the young lady feeling okay?"

"Let's get out," begged Laura.

"No dice. You can't find another taxi in Buenos Aires at this hour."

"Don't you worry now. I really won't be long . . . and it is such a beautiful afternoon. If you wish I could take you to the Costanera on the River Plate. There are such nice open-air restaurants where you can eat a steak and enjoy a cool bottle of beer. Buenos Aires is lovely in fall, right? The air is so soft, just like springtime."

"This guy is nuts," said Pablo getting furious.

Laura snuggled up to him. "Where in God's name is he taking us?"

The taxi turned onto Sarmiento Street and stopped in front of a gate.

"I'm just going to be gone five minutes. Please excuse me. Here are some magazines so you won't get bored; and for you, young lady, this delicious piece of chocolate. It's all porous, like a honeycomb."

The taxi came to rest in a courtyard surrounded by apartments with tall doors and half hidden by ferns.

"Maybe he brought us to another hotel. Please, not here," begged Laura, "I refuse to do it here."

"Please, just five minutes," the man repeated as he left the car. He walked over to one of the doors and opened it quickly. Trombones and trumpets blared out from the open door giving the impression of a Mardi Gras band.

"Brothers," a voice cried out, "I've been a sinner, but I repent my sins before all of you now and on Sunday I'll do it again, as a testimonial."

"Please, let's get out of here," she demanded.

"Don't worry. These loonies belong to one of these evangelical cults," answered Pablo, quite relieved.

"Oh, Lord, save us and have pity on this corrupt flesh," a voice exclaimed behind the door.

"Laura rested her head on Pablo's shoulder. He put his arm around her waist and began to kiss her. After a few minutes the taxi driver returned with a woman in uniform. He started laughing. "See, I told you I'd be back in a hurry. Goodbye, sister; see you Sunday."

He awkwardly maneuvered the car out of the patio.

"So it's still the Hotel Azul, is it?"Without waiting for an answer, he went on: "Beautiful afternoon, right? Are you sure you want to spend your time in there? Is the young lady feeling better? Really, to lock yourselves in a dark room on a golden afternoon like this . . . "

When the old taxi finally arrived at the hotel the porte-cochère entrance was closed.

"They are filled up. Shall we drive around the block? It is always like this. As soon as a car leaves they open the gate. It's like a trap."

"Yes, yes, go around the block," stammered Laura.

The old Ford kept on circling the block. Laura lost count: five, six, eight, ten? Somehow she felt that her life consisted of a continuous circling around one block or another, wearing out the asphalt that had already been worn thin by countless cars turning around and around waiting for the gate to open.

The next time around another car just beat them to the open entrance.

"Ride around some more?" The driver laughed again. "Maybe you finally changed your minds and want to go elsewhere? . . . Certainly a most beautiful afternoon. Maybe you are in the mood to go for a walk in Palermo Park . . . or go to the movies. That's it, the movies. In the Flower Palace they are showing *Music from Heaven.* Have you seen it?"

"Just keep on circling," snapped Pablo, "and cut out the chatter."

"Will we ever stop going around in circles?" asked Laura, almost in tears.

"Just be patient. This always happens."

Laura saw herself as a child again, riding on the merry-go-round on Plaza Vicente Lopez until her mother motioned her from the window to come home. And that motion was a sign constituting a personal, sacred message which was really meant for some phantom or monster materializing out of nowhere, ready to swallow her up.

"It's always like this," repeated Pablo, "we'll make it yet."

"Yes, sometimes we have circled up to thirty rounds. Took almost a whole hour. What fun." The man at the wheel laughed again and this time turned to look at them.

"Let's get out," said Laura, almost in a whisper.

"Just keep on circling," ordered Pablo while squeezing her arm. "Just go on as long as you have to."

"Okay, okay, don't get sore. Usually something funny happens while circling like this . . . have you ever gone around the block on roller skates?"

The taxi kept on moving. Every time the closed gate came in sight Pablo squeezed Laura's arm and she rested her body against him. The driver counted off the turns, almost triumphantly. "Nine . . . what did I tell you . . . nine times already."

Then his tone of voice changed. "We could try somewhere else. I could take you to the Dietzel Hotel. It's a pretty one."

"No, it has to be here, here, you understand?" Pablo's voice sounded angry. The Ford kept on going.

"This hotel is quite strange. As if somebody blessed it," the driver added with a laugh. "Once our group came here with Sister Benigna who also happens to be my wife. You met her. And here she became pregnant. After ten years, pregnant."

"We aren't interested in your sex life; just drive on."

"No, leave him be . . . let him talk . . . ," protested Laura.

"Well, we came here to do some good. After we got in we slipped the message of our brother Erwin Jefferson underneath all the closed doors when nobody was looking . . . well, and then we had some time for ourselves and we were blessed for our efforts. My wife got pregnant after ten years . . . a miracle, wouldn't you think?"

This time the gate as open.

"Quickly, inside," commanded Pablo with an anguished voice.

Laura straightened up until her body became rigid.

"All right," said the driver sadly.

The taxi stopped. A reddish light shone mutedly on their faces. A short man opened the car door.

"Now don't be scared. Nobody here knows you." Pablo continued with a smile: "And you won't run into your father like it happens in those Russian novels."

"I don't have a father," replied Laura bitterly.

"So long, young lady. Do you want me to wait outside? Don't forget to look under the rug next to the door."

Nobody answered him. The corridor led to a hallway with a staircase covered by a red carpet. There were doors up and down the hall.

'Upstairs,' thought Laura, 'it would be easier upstairs . . . ' But the man led them to one of the doors on the main floor.

"Take off your coat," said Pablo, trying to find something to say.

Laura was not listening. Instead she began to roam around the room. She opened drawers that were totally empty; she pushed back curtains that covered up walls simulating windows. Pablo watched her every move.

"And now what?" He tried to sound superior and very manly.

Laura inspected a contraption on which to rest the shoe while undoing it. Then she lifted the rug next to the door and began to laugh hysterically while letting her head drop on the edge of the bed.

The silence of the room was being filled with her sobs. Pablo had remained motionless, his back turned to her.

"I don't force anybody to come here, you understand? I don't want any explanations either. All you've done today is complain. I've had it with you. We're leaving. All that damned taxi driver's fault . . ."

Laura dragged herself over to the sink. She made the water run really hard so as not to hear his words.

"These things only happen to me . . . ," groaned Pablo. "Never got a chance to get anything going. That's what happens to me for getting involved with liberal arts students."

When they arrived at her boarding house, Laura spoke first. "Please excuse my behavior. I don't quite understand myself what happened to me. Maybe another day."

"I'll accompany you upstairs."

A narrow and badly lit staircase led to the second floor. The steps seemed to be endless, one fitting into the next like an escalator. They never seemed to end. Perhaps they belonged to a circular staircase leading to an abyss filled with darkness.

"When will we meet again?" he asked putting his arm around her.

They had reached the last step, and Laura felt an icy shiver running down her spine, as cold as the imitation marble floor.

"Forgive me," he said, "I'd never imagined that it was the first time for you. Why didn't you tell me? From now on I want to see you every day. There aren't many girls like you left these days."

Laura turned the key in her lock. She did not even wait to see him descend the stairs, barely visible in the light of the match he had struck to light his cigarette.

'I'll have to move out of here tomorrow,' was the first thought that came to her mind. 'I'll never want to see him again.' She sat down on the floor without turning on the lights. As she put her hands in the pockets of her jacket she came upon the piece of chocolate that the man from the Salvation Army had given her. She slowly began to eat it, suppressing her sobs.

Takeover
Beatriz Guido

In the beginning, in the very beginning, I travelled once a week from Buenos Aires to Azul. I always stopped in the outskirts of town, at the Progreso cafe to drink a cup of coffee when it was cold or a glass of draft beer in summer. This was my way of getting ready to take the resurfaced road of Alma Muerta and to come face to face with Las Acacias. I am talking about facing Las Acacias because I know the end of the story, and it can no longer be written any other way. Las Acacias represented the richest farm land in the area, and I had inherited it because my family was beset with a procreation problem that bordered on the miraculous in bad luck. I was an only son in a family of seven brothers who had married several times looking in vain for male descendants and who could not even produce as much as a faulty pregnancy or an abortion. They decided against adoptions, maybe because they saw me as a sort of miracle, vaguely tied to their flesh and blood, imagining that I reincarnated the tenacious will to maintain the family name at all costs.

As a child I had learned to display for each of them an overwhelming demonstration of affection. I forced them to come to my birthday party or High School celebration and I left my most fascinating games in order to be bored by their presence. I never forgot their Saint's day, I laughed or cried according to the type of story they told me, and I carried their polo trophies around the house as if it were a holy procession. I managed to stay on the good side of all of them. There were tears in our goodbyes and tenderness blossomed on post cards sent from abroad. My parents had the good taste of dying early, thus giving me the coveted status of an orphan which made all of them feel so responsible towards me. And they represented Las Acacias. There was no dispute over the will, no doubt over the ownership. The place was mine, all mine, from the moment that my oldest uncle, Nicasio, was shot by a farmhand in the Southern part of

75

the province, an event that kept him confined to a wheelchair. "One of those unfortunate things," people said, and everybody blamed Perón. But nothing was ever mentioned about it thereafter.

From that day on I offered to leave Law School—it had taken me two years to pass the entrance exam—and take charge of Las Acacias. My uncles felt sorry for me, thought how hard it would be to deal with the hired hands, and made out the will while they were all still alive.

But they also showed me their wisdom, prudence, foresight and intuition by introducing me to my wife-to-be, Maria Inés, blood of my blood, supposedly a shirt-tail relative. At least I did not have to pretend to be happy with her. I fell in love with her mysterious gestures, her golden face, and the delicate way with which she wore English tweeds, cashmere sweaters and the natural pink pearls that had belonged to my mother. She laughed dutifully when I told stories to entertain my uncles and kept a virtuous silence while we made love.

Of course we had no children. This we accepted as a sign decreed by fate. She never insisted on seeing a gynecologist or a country quack. Once in a while I surprised her looking at the figure of a child on the cover of a magazine that she quickly hid away.

In those days we travelled a lot. I had purchased some fine Charolais bulls in Europe, and that gave me a chance to take Maria Inés to Paris so that she could visit Givenchy or Casini and spend the afternoons at Rumplemayer's while I had the Charolais loaded into the iron belly of the Conte Grande. It was fun to travel with prized animals on a steamship and watch them during the crossing. It was also an opportunity to go below deck with friends and show them what the future meat supply of the famous La Cabaña restaurant in Buenos Aires would look like. They would surely end up there.

I said that I went almost every week to Las Acacias. I usually spent a night and on the following afternoon took the train back to Buenos Aires. I used to sit on the West porch in a big wicker chair with a fancy fan-like design on the back. I had stopped riding horseback since the time my feet got tangled up in the stirrups and the blasted horse paraded me around the polo field before a crowd in the bleachers. Although I was not injured I could never get over the shame and humiliation of that day; after all, this very animal had amassed trophies for my happy uncles.

The problems of Las Acacias came to me by way of the general manager, Padilla, who usually took care of them. His father, his grandfather, and his great-grandfather had served our family since the

Indian wars in times of General Roca. The Padillas seldom went to town. I remembered hearing my father say: "Some day we ought to give them the deed to the house they live in or the land around it." But nothing was ever done, and the Padillas never pressed the matter. In fact, during the most difficult times of the Perón regime they turned out to be more protective of the land than the owner and joined the old conservative party in Azul to show their loyalty.

An apparently uncanny coincidence or misfortune had brought the Padillas closer to me—that is what I used to think then—due to the fact that their children were all girls. Padilla's six daughters had managed to turn him into a surly and ruminating man. He impressed me with his unique brand of homespun philosophy as he reported about the financial state of the farm including the registered death and birth of the animals. The estate was actually flourishing due to favorable weather and the new farm policy of the governments that, after the fall of Perón, became convinced that the true riches of our country originated in the land, the blessed, rolling prairie land of the Buenos Aires province.

But let me return to Aristobulo Padilla: he was given that name to honor my grandfather. He was a man of about forty-five, neither tall nor short. He had small eyes, a thin mouth, and big, deformed hands that were used to deliver a calf or swing a whip to tame colts as well as punish his daughters. The latter constituted Aristobulo Padilla's tragedy: "What are those females good for? The whorehouse or some macho who comes and takes them along with him . . . " Sometimes, about the time when the day turns into dusk, he felt the need to unburden himself with me.

"To think that one's own flesh and blood, one's daughter, is nothing but a body to be enjoyed by somebody else. To think that they were born and educated so that they can provide pleasure for some man. You are lucky, Don Marcelo, that your wife never got pregnant. What if it had been a girl? Why didn't I drown mine when they were born, like you do with kittens." Once he really let himself go, saying: "If they had been males everything would be different; this land could be mine now." But he quickly caught himself and tried to cover up. "Lucky for your father and all your uncles that you came along. Otherwise, what would have become of Las Acacias!"

Las Acacias! Perhaps the choicest piece of land in the southern part of the whole province, surrounded by two hundred parcels of tenant farms that belonged to the estate; one dominant colonial mansion with huge porches, tall Doric columns and balustrades on the terrace. Its color had always been pink, just the way Basualdo had painted it not long ago, that picture now hanging in the main dining room that was always closed and with chairs clustered around the table, waiting for their only guests: phantoms or witches who would come at midnight, because the house was made to accommodate specters. Never, not even in its heydey, had the place been inhabited. Its owners had lived and died in Paris or London, and that went on for generations. Sometimes it served as a home for a convalescent, nothing more.

When I returned from my trip the help prepared the bedroom that I had used as a child, next to the servants' quarters. During those short weekly stays I ate with the help.

I don't rightfully remember when they told me—mumbling something about the humidity seeping through the walls—that they had prepared the master bedroom for me in which my parents had slept. I remember that it was a sultry summer night; pink gauze covered the tall mahogany bedposts and heightened the strange beauty of this room that looked like an eternal bridal suite.

A strange uneasiness came over me as I began to play the role of the traveller who had come home after all these years. Every sound that reached me caused a special sensation: the tinkling of the glass in the chandelier, the song of the crickets and the cries of the *tero* birds and the magpies in the marshes. Through the window bars and screens barn owls were watching me.

I undressed in the dark and slipped between the linen sheets, cooler and smoother than I remembered. For the first time I felt sorry not to have Maria Inés at my side. She got car-sick so easily, and neither one of us liked to fly, especially that local route to the South. I usually did not sleep in the nude. You catch cold that way, they used to warn me as a child. But tonight I had turned out the light because of the mosquitoes and then could not find my pajamas. Feeling my naked body against the cool sheets took me back to my childhood: memories of solitary, fortuitous pleasures that faded away and became replaced by others as my uncles took care to provide me with young servant girls or deluxe prostitutes that kept my insomnia at bay.

I tossed around in my bed; twice to the right, once to the left. The matrimonial bed loomed wide, soft and flat. Turning over again to the left I came upon a bare, warm body. An embrace followed, accompanied by a fragrance, the unmistakable smell of freshly baked bread. My hand—at first paralyzed by the initial shock—began to discover that passive, motionless nakedness. I had no intention of turning on the light and finding out what kind of a face went with this body. I was afraid that this creature might vanish or be burned by the light like a moth or a firefly. My hand responded to a movement of her head. Her hair began to cover my chest like the initial step of a strange ritual. My hands attempted in vain to identify her. Then I did decide to turn on the light, but her arm stopped me and her lips began to run across my chest following an established order. From then on I only remember falling into an abyss of unsuspected dimensions. Her body pressed against mine, tense and vibrant; it was young and expert at the same time, virginal and all-knowing. I started to fall into a deep sleep in which reality and fantasy were intertwined.

I awoke as the sunlight was hitting my pillow. My hand started a quick search between the sheets. Only the smell of freshly baked bread remained and the cozy feeling left behind by a warm body that had just gotten out of bed.

I had my breakfast in the kitchen feeling like a hungry, sad and ill-tempered animal. I sensed that I had fallen into the trap of an infantile and erotic dream. I quickly left for Buenos Aires without even trying to find out what kind of servant girls were living on the estate.

During the next week I walked the streets of the big city in silence. I was not worried about having deceived Maria Inés but feared to have fallen prey to a kind of sorcery. I began to count the days and then the hours until it was time to return to Las Acacias.

As soon as I arrived at the estate I took my seat in the porch and waited for Padilla. I quickly signed the necessary checks, listened to his tales of woe about the hoof and mouth disease and the locusts, skipped dinner, went to bed and waited, first with the lights on, then in the dark. The crickets, *tero* birds and barn owls were back. Later on I dozed off. Turning again on my left side, I felt a body next to mine, naked, tranquil, confident. This one did not have the fragrance of freshly baked bread but rather smelled like rain water, like hair washed in rain water. My first impulse led me to turn on the light but a firm arm stopped me. This time my desire rose to an unsuspected height. I let myself be carried away again by the expert and yet virginal flesh while the copious, soft hair unfolded on my chest.

She had her way with me like the last time; after arousing my passion several times and not answering my questions—I was beginning to feel more and more grateful for falling into a kind of erotic abyss that made me feel for the first time like swimming in a fertile sea of happiness—she left me in a deep sleep. I no longer was even interested to find out who she was because I felt afraid that she would disappear permanently. I rather contented myself with being part of a sorcery or a strange bewitchment, playing my assigned role in the re-enactment of a legend or the caprice of a divine mistress in what by now seemd to be a historic bed. I conveniently forgot that my parents had inherited this same bed and that I might have been conceived in it. At any rate, I no longer tried to turn on the light.

This time I woke up a happy man. I breakfasted on the porch and listened to Padilla's confidences while already thinking about the next visit. I did not dare to stay a second night, afraid that the repetition might break the enchantment.

I spent the week in Buenos Aires filling my days with all kinds of useless chores to kill the time. I also increased my affection for Maria Inés and my uncles because I felt a need to return some of the great joy that had invaded my whole being.

And so I spent the next few months, always finding her on my left, always a different enchantress: sage, precise, crafty, offering and denying herself in the game of love, always exuding a different fragrance, alternating between the oven-fresh bread, well water, wet grass and anisette biscuits. Sometimes the hair was put up, other times loose or straight; at times her skin was electrified by a fresh breeze, other times it was smooth and soft, like peach fuzz. Once I got alarmed because my hands seemed to feel a certain roundness of the belly, but that only increased my ardor and made me forget any thoughts.

Then came the trip to Europe. Padilla needed to crossbreed the newest Charolais with the original breed so that we might send an animal to be exhibited at the *Sociedad Rural* in early winter.

I forgot to explain that by now he was in charge of the estate. I had left him a power-of-attorney so as not to spend valuable time signing checks and papers. This procedure gave me more free time to go to my room in the early afternoon and wait for the gust of darkness and the miraculous apparition, the incarnation of my blood's longing.

I left for Europe feeling anxious and unsure of myself. Some power had taken control of me denying me any measure of happiness outside of Las Acacias. But, inspite of that, my trip lasted several months. Sitting in the drawing room of the Prince of Wales Hotel my adventure took on the shape of a fantastic story, something right out of the pages of Borges or Bioy Casares, whose lands bordered on mine. I began to feel ashamed of myself and even began to suspect that the ranch help had played a heavy joke on me. But as soon as I landed in Buenos Aires I quickly greeted my uncles and flew a Piper Cub to Las Acacias.

There was no sign of Padilla or any of the ranch hands. I felt elated and rushed to my room. All I could do was to wait.

She came to me again that night; I held her in my arms and pressed my body against hers while she laughed and laughed, no longer afraid of being recognized.

The next morning I was awakened by the crying, shouting and howling of several babies. I left the room in a state of alarm trying to trace the cries. In the wicker chairs of the porch, bundled up like the babies of remote and invented ancestors that stared at me from the pictures in the living room, I counted four, five, six babies who in spite of their contorted faces easily showed a very white, transparent skin that betrayed a total resemblance to my features.

I ran to the kitchen but found it empty. It was in the dining room that I found Padilla's six daughters. Their laughter followed me throughout the house. I ran into them everywhere, spying on me behind doors while the children, my children, were lying on the shelves and the tables, between the porcelain cats and the Sèvres china. It was only then that I realized that they all had taken over the house and maybe the land and that Las Acacias did not belong to me anymore.

MARTA LYNCH

Born in the Argentine capital in 1930, Marta Lynch studied liberal arts at the University of Buenos Aires. In the first post-Perón era she worked with a small group of radical intellectuals and writers to elect Arturo Frondizi to the presidency, although he was later toppled by a military coup d'état. Her first novel, *La alfombra roja* (1962), is considered by critics to be a *roman a clef* that describes the devious and ruthless world of politics, focusing on the complex personality of the presidential candidate.

Three years later, her second novel, *Al vencedor,* gives further proof of the author's involvement with national issues and realities. Through the eyes of the narrator, a young soldier from the interior, the reader discovers a bitterly divided Argentina saturated with moral decay, class struggle and civic indifference, the legacy of the Perón years that would culminate a few years later in guerilla warfare and renewed military dictatorships. In her third novel, *La señora Ordóñez* (1968), Marta Lynch turns to the problem of unrequited love and frustrated sex, a theme repeated in many of her later works, especially her short stories. Told with great candor and sexual explicitness that shocked the Argentine bourgeois reader of the time, the novel centers around the life of a mature woman who cannot escape her marital bonds due to her dependence on her husband and who takes a lover to overcome an otherwise meaningless existence.

In the 1970's Lynch became an outstanding story writer, managing to interpret female-male relationships with unerring humor, irony, and, at

83

times, pathos. In a number of these stories, society is featured very prominently as a background providing incentives derived from the mass culture that pervades the big-city milieu. In the title story of *Bedtime Story* the young female narrator adroitly plays the role of a sex object in order to climb the ladder of success to beauty contests, television appearances and film contracts in a male-dominated world. "Latin Lover," somewhat more autobiographical, reveals the ironic attitude of the narrator who consciously plays the traditional role of the kept woman for a man whom she loved, until the realization of her demeaning condition causes her to shut a final door.

BIBLIOGRAPHY

La alfombra roja, 1962 (novel)
Al vencedor, 1965 (novel)
Los cuentos tristes, 1966 (stories)
La señora Ordóñez, 1968 (novel)
Cuentos de colores, 1970 (stories)
El cruce del rio, 1972 (novel)
Un arbol lleno de manzanas, 1974 (novel)
Los dedos de la mano, 1976 (stories)
La penúltima versión de la Colorado Villanueva, 1978 (novel)

Bedside Story

Marta Lynch

My grandmother, sitting in the doorway of her house, had always told me that I'd go far in the world and pointed at the intersection of Bocayuava and Yrigoyen; sometimes she'd get even more enthusiastic and motioned towards the big artery of Castro Barros. That was far for her. Listening to her and feeling like the center of attraction I stopped in my childish games to take in the looks and the leers of the neighbors, especially grandmother's boarders who all predicted that I'd make it big some day.

Thinking back on those days I recall that even then I was what they call a real beauty what with my large, light-colored eyes and my thick black hair that mother let me grow long before it became the fashion. I do have a sister, but she couldn't compare with me at all. I think it happens a lot that in a family there is one outstanding beauty, somebody exotic, and that it is the duty of all the other members to treat her accordingly. My sister used to tell me: "Gladys, you're a real beaut." When she and I took our clothes off in the locker room at the social club or in our living room where we both slept on hide-away beds, she used to give me long, hard stares filled with curiosity and envy.

At fourteen I was a long-legged beauty with breasts that pointed upward without the help of a bra. My sister Elvira was far from being an ugly duckling, but she took after mother in being short and a little on the broad side. Like the other married women in the neighborhood, mother took up knitting after lunch and waited for the soap operas to come on TV. But she worried about me. Everyone in the *barrio* seemed to notice me, and on Saturday afternoons when we went to the club mother observed how the people around me stopped talking in order to give me the once-over. And to think that there I won my first beauty contest. It was Mardi Gras time and I had not quite turned seventeen when the club's president who owned a barber shop called me in.

85

"Gladys," he said, all excited—I had begun to notice that men like him get all tangled up inside when facing a pretty girl like me; in fact, they almost drool—"Gladys, this contest is tailor-made for you. For all purposes . . . " He stopped there.

I started to wonder about that "for all purposes," and so I smartly asked him what he meant. He simply babbled something about me being a shoo-in, but I wanted to know who else would be competing. There was Leonor, for instance, the daughter of a postman; we practically threw poisoned darts at each other when we met at the grocery store or the local movie theater; and Esther who worked in a soda bottling plant and who was a little bow-legged but pretty otherwise; and then Irma who had quit a good job as a salesgirl in order to work in some office where she could sit all day because standing up eight hours a day can give you varicose veins.

Dad, who had just been promoted by the municipality, insisted on knowing all the details about the beauty contest such as having to parade around in tight bathing suits or having the jurors take my measurements like they do in the movies. Daddy had these silly scruples when I was already a perfect 36-24-36, which at seventeen is quite a feat and, if you think about it, the most important pre-requisite for a woman. And I dare anybody to dispute that. Even my school principal, a somewhat sad woman who had known me since second grade, had to admit that I was right.

When we met on the street she told me: "Only a sixth-grade education, Gladys? You'll have a hard time finding a job. Nowadays people demand an education and knowledge . . . "

We were talking on the corner of Boedo Avenue across from the school and the light from the pizzeria hit my sweater just right while I saw the reflection of my raven hair in the window. There wasn't a man going by who didn't turn his fool head and some even stopped pretending to light a match or glance at the magazines in the news stand. The principal might have been sad, but she was far from blind. "You'll get along all right," she decided.

I got rid of her because I knew that I'd win the beauty contest and I didn't want any spoilsports. I quit after sixth grade because, in spite of my being prettier, Esther always wound up with the best parts in the school plays because she had such a phenomenal memory. As for myself, I had the hardest time even memorizing a poem and I seriously began to have doubts about my movie career.

My sister and I used to talk endlessly about leading male roles for me, the clothes we'd need, seeing my name in big letters on the marquee, and the fabulous pay that would allow us to move to Barrio Norte or downtown, at least far away from this crummy neighborhood. Since my waist was getting smaller and my breasts were pointing upward all by themselves, I finally decided to become a model, and so I spent my time walking around with a book on my head while holding my stomach in. About this time mother began to get used to the idea that one of her daughters might be using her natural assets for something beyond domestic bliss. She began to back up my dreams and used all the spending money to buy fashion magazines while the seamstress down the street got really excited about making clothes for an authentic Argentine 36-24-36.

Finally the contest was to be in sweater and skirt because Leonor's father threatened to go to the Juvenile Court and the local priest put pressure on the school; and so we showed up on Sunday the fifteenth of February as the heat was melting the asphalt and the sky looked as if it was going to burst with rain. Our clubhouse was packed and everyone was waiting for the barbecue and dance after the contest.

We paraded up and down in the banquet hall and I remember that my new shoes hurt like hell. Following the advice of my mother and the beauty expert from the drugstore at Castro Barros and Yrigoyen, I sucked in my guts and pushed out my breasts as far as they would go. All around us the crowd was dense and whispering, the women giving us a critical once-over and the guys eating us up with their eyes. Summoning up all my modelling know-how, I tried to strike an original pose, but now that I've been in this business for a while I realize how awkward I must have looked, even to those simple souls from my *barrio*, me in those tight, new shoes and the skirt that reached down to my calves. But after the turn I knew that I'd won because the president and the radio writer on the jury looked at me wild-eyed. Both of them were practically jumping out of their skin jotting down things on a greenish paper. I thought I was going to faint when everybody converged on me, and the president announced that I was the new queen while mother was trying to get a glass of water for me although she seemed more interested in the prize money than my present state of health which had never been better.

The other girls sort of made themselves scarce as fast as possible because the taste of defeat must have been a pretty bitter pill to swallow, although I had not experienced it as yet.

That was my first night of glory. From then on I paraded before the public in my bathing suit while other girls showed themselves in skirts and sweaters; and so I went from one contest to another. And then there was that radio writer. Well, I had been fooling around since I was fifteen with a certain boy in the *barrio* who worked in a tire factory and studied English in his spare time. He was quite good-looking although he usually bored me to tears. He was an honest kid who claimed he loved me. One Saturday afternoon as we sat in the last row of the movie house, neither one of us watched the screen, and after a while things got to be sizzling and we wound up in a hotel room on Rioja Street. But Pedro—that was his name—never quite understood that a body like mine belonged to the world. In that sense the radio writer was much smarter because he realized that he had to promote his merchandise if he was going to get a piece of the action. Even the president of the club understood these fundamentals, although I had to satisfy his urges in the very office where he had crowned me queen; but I thought it best just to give in a little rather than to make an enemy.

Returning to the writer, I had to admit that so far in my career I owe him a lot; he has done his best to look out for a girl's interests once she played ball with him. So I told Pedro who by now wanted to marry me to get lost and immediately entered every beauty contest I could find: the Miss Springtime, Mardi Gras, Villa Urquiza and even the one of the Uruguayan community in Buenos Aires. I was a smashing success. By this time I had gotten used to the routine of squeezing into my bathing suit, putting on the high heels and even posing for the girlie magazine in which I appeared each month.

The court of my admirers grew steadily as the photos, the publicity and the beauty contests brought me the applause of the men and looks that could kill from all the women. But my sister stuck by me. She seemed to get a kick out of my taking off my clothes, posing for a picture or winning another prize. Confiding in my mother—I don't see dad much anymore—I remember telling her that I wanted to be an actress and how it bothered me when a lady who was a big shot on one of those juries tried to find out why I wanted to be in the contest at all. I looked her in the face without knowing what she meant. She was ugly, gloomy and old; at least that's how she looked to me, and I figured that she was jealous of my being so popular. But she just sat there snuggly in her fur coat and those big, sad eyes of hers that looked a bit like mine, asking: "What is it that makes you enter these contests?"

My looks, old gal, my looks and my being nineteen, I should have answered; but instead I just smiled.

"I want to be an actress," I said with my celebrated, throaty voice, "an actress."

A few people around me smiled.

"Well, all right, " said the old hag, "but that should give you a feeling of security and happiness, a feeling of responsibility towards your beauty."

Feeling of responsibility. Nobody is going to feel less responsible than a beautiful nineteen year old woman who is free to do what she pleases, who is chased by every pair of pants in town, wrapped up in a cloud of male ardor wherever she goes.

"You're really something," said my writer when he got out of bed in his apartment, "really something else."

I sort of cared for the guy although neither one of us ever tried to find out what exactly was the thing we had going between us, whether it was what they call love or some other stupid reason. He was really good in making contacts for me in television, and so I began to follow a pretty tough schedule of dressing up in an evening gown about noon in order to appear for a minute and a half before the cameras at 2:15 together with a top-notch model who was the star of the show. But I waited patiently for those two-and-a-half hours sipping tea and munching dry toast in the coffee shop while my sister put little touches on my heavy make-up and arranged my sequin-covered dress. But some nights I could hardly walk because my feet felt swollen and my eyes hurt from the glare. I was always half-starved and had to endure insults and give in to the vulgar demands of the studio executives, always hoping to make the right connection. My writer did what he could and almost got me into the movies; but he and I were just small fries for those big fish in the movie industry, and all we came up with were some married technicians or a few young camera operators who just earned enough to take me out on pay day. So it was back to the commercials for me, gulping down some pop for two seconds or holding up an empty can of olive oil. And that's when I told my writer that I planned to go back to my beloved beauty contests even if there wasn't much future in it. I could only think of those precious seconds when I would parade up and down the aisle with all eyes staring like hypnotized at my vital parts and the feeling of the gilded metal crown slowly being pushed down on my black, silky curls. I even thought that one of these times the president of the contest might turn out to be a kind but very influential man who would help me along. My writer didn't like the idea one bit and got really sore before leaving me all dolled up for the famous minute and a half before the TV cameras at 2:15. He said a lot of horrible things about my mother and sister, and just to show him that I could make it on my own I registered that same afternoon for the Miss Argentina contest.

The next fifteen days turned out to be pretty hectic. The things one had to do to be considered a perfect body.

"You are an authentic 36-24½ (by now)-36," said my sister who had changed a lot and now insisted on being my manager.

Things did get a little tough when the real competition showed up. Leonor and Marina were two gals who knew how to get to the top. Marina was a professional model, already twenty-nine, been married and had a child that was being taken care of by her mother, a friendly woman who wanted her daughter to win as badly as mine did. None of us met her husband but we all knew that Marina was in love with Ezquivel, a portrait photographer. That was Marina's big triumph. She had photos that made your eyes pop and she used one of them so effectively that her husband slashed his wrists in front of the Durand Hospital. My sister thought it was good for the competition to run into trouble because it takes away some of the glamor. Marina looked awfully dejected every night from then on sitting with her group, a real odd bunch that included an unpublished poet one day and a used car salesman the next, plus people from the ad agencies, all in all a strange world in miniature that nobody could make out. As far as Leonor was concerned, I'd just have to say that she was as full of lies and tricks as when I ran into her during my first contest in the neighborhood club. But she and her gang showed a suspicious confidence although during the last year I had been winning the smaller contests such as the panty-hose one, the woolen sweater one, Miss Channel Ten and Miss Mar del Plata. But Leonor had learned how to get on the good side of the P.R. guys and even struck up a friendship with the famous Maciel who had married a theater actress and showed up in all the magazines. Leonor made the semi-finals, and by that time mother, sister and I got the hunch that Leonor, Marina and yours truly would be the ones to slug it out in the end. It sure wasn't easy getting through those last few weeks waiting for the big finale, what with being forced to live with each other, having to flash that constant smile and drinking tomato juice and eating nothing but boiled rice, partly as a beauty treatment and partly because I was broke by that time. I got so tired of rubbing elbows with the competition day in and day out, and between the two of them they drove me batty. Marina at least showed some character by leaning on the men for support which was reasonable, and my mother agreed with me on that one. But Leonor with her gangly, little salesgirl's voice was hiding invitations and messing up the make-up kit just before we needed it, and that was hard to swallow. We hardly spoke to each other any longer.

Then I had to endure Mrs. Armel, the owner of Armel Cosmetics who was showing a special personal interest in us; but I put her in her place because in my book it takes a boy and a girl to make a couple, even if Mrs. Armel carried a basketful of money and influence.

One afternoon I couldn't stand the whole thing any longer and broke down crying so hard that Leonor came over and I used the opportunity to slap her face real good. Leonor started yelling so loud that the cop, the fireman and the receptionist from downstairs rushed up. Then I really found out what it means to be involved with the world of television, beauty contests and its backers. Money and looks really make the world go round. Well, they all rushed in just about when Leonor and I were trying to claw each other with the faint hope of settling the contest right there and then. But the fireman used his persuasion backed up by his muscles to pull us apart. From that moment on life got to be pretty miserable and I lost three pounds without the aid of tomato juice and long walks in the neighborhood.

All along I had to force myself to stop thinking about what went with the first prize. Lots of money, trips, a fur coat, a week in the most deluxe hotel in California, another week in Madrid, and a final week at the fancy Alvear Palace Hotel where the final contest was being held. And from then on, just riding the crest of the wave. I don't know why that saying of my mother always appealed to me. Riding the crest of the wave as if glory equalled riding a fiery stallion that would take me to the land of milk and honey. My beauty would finally become my passport to happiness and I'd ride the wave to the glittering marquee with my name flashing on it; and it would mean goodbye to all this shabbiness, the long wait while nursing a tea and dry biscuits, the rummaging through the bargain basements for the cheapest dress, the walking in worn-out shoes, and the sliding into the Coupe de Ville of some fat and demanding character with connections. It would be goodbye to the whole stinking rat race; and then the day of the final contest came. Now that I look back at it, I must confess that everything went so fast that I hardly remember much. There we were with the goods: stuck-out breasts, almond eyes, solid legs and rounded behinds: ready for action. Some of the contestants were making religious vows and I saw a girl from Ciudadela take a crucifix out of her purse and kiss it repeatedly. Some of the mothers accompanied their girls right up to the stage, and in a flash I saw the grim expression on my mother's and sister's faces transformed into a sort of angelic glow as I appeared. Someone pinched my thigh and then we were blinded by the glaring lights, and the stares and voices of the public began to blend into a grand, indistinguishable totality. I felt like a bullfighter in the center of the ring. They called us by name and number.

As we took our turns the smell, the murmur and the shouting of the crowd increased.

It is strange to think back about it now, but Leonor won and Marina cried her eyes out. I didn't shed a tear. After all, I am what they've told me all along: a knockout, and I think that my day will yet come. For right now it was a matter of staying calm. Taking advantage of the rules I went back to my luxury suite, ordered coq-au-vin and a bottle of ice-cold champagne and charged it to Ardel Cosmetics. I ate until I was stuffed and settled down to thinking that tomorrow would be early enough to look for another beauty contest or follow up on a few connections that I had made. There's nothing like owning a beautiful body if you know what I mean. And my mother and sister, sipping their champagne, fully agreed.

Latin Lover

Marta Lynch

At first I thought that it was a joke, but suddenly I knew. He made his decision as soon as he had finished inspecting the apartment and proceeded to hand me the keys. Surrounded by chairs with nylon covers and flowers made out of plastic he ventured a slight gesture of displeasure: look at it this way, he told me, it's camp. He might just as well have said *crash* or *toc,* but he said *camp* and it made me retreat within myself remembering that awkward poem of his that talks about congenital coldness.

Well, all right, the nylon, the plastic flowers and the narrow bed would start being my home. The living room was flooded with light coming in through a tall window barely covered by colored curtains that matched the nylon and the ashtray. The ashtray was blue, made out of clay and had the *campy* shape of a toilet seat. By the time he returned from looking at the kitchen I had stuck the ashtray under a pillow, but he lifted the pillow and saw it. He always finds everything. We decided to keep the ashtray, and then he said: it's not a bad place, and I moved in. From now on my life would take place in a campy living room-dining room combination, a bathroom, kitchen and patio. Most of the windows were too high to allow a view of the street except the one in the bedroom. From here I could see the terraces of adjacent buildings and a busy street.

He was eager to fit my existence into these campy rooms and did so with the best of intentions, the ones he reserved for things that did not cost too much of an effort. His hazel eyes wore a neutral expression; neither cold nor discouraging, just mere eyes. I had adored these eyes with a fervor that showed in my slightest gestures. At times I thought that such fervor had overwhelmed him, but, then again, I have my doubts. I am ready to admit that he seemed happy enough with letting himself be adored. But

93

here I have to be fair: he adored me too, only just once in a while. Well, nobody is going to pretend that a man and woman are going to meet at the same corner at exactly the same time. Maybe I harbored some doubts when that apartment business started, but I only managed to complain weakly, like somebody stuck all alone in a dark elevator. Alarm bells went off all over inside of me and then a feeling of anxiety began to spread through my being. I was able to formulate my fear about being afraid all by myself in the middle of the night, but the words just floated upwards and were left hanging on the bronze table lamps.

And so my new life began. One might have thought that the whole situation was exceedingly difficult, but it was not. That was the devilish thing about it all, it was so easy. In fact, I could see myself continuing in this situation until the day I would die of a ripe old age. That kind of a love relationship turns into a vicious circle, and we are left to look in on it from the outside. Maybe he taught me that trick.

I had never met a man who acted more like a person in transit; in fact, I felt like handing him his suitcase every time he left. To tell the truth, his life was so predictable that I could imagine it step by step. So many hours at work, so many at his home, so many in the car, and so many for me. He never came out and talked about it. That was due to his delicate nature. He never would have been able to take the initiative to say goodbye to me. But then again, we were both treading water in the middle of the river and would and could not stop now, what with the apartment, the plastic flowers and the prison-like windows.

During the first two days I tried to get rid of the prison smell. He did not seem to care one way or the other about that. We made love. Badly. That can happen. The very first time it is bad no matter where. It also happens when moving into a new place. We have made love in hotels, a car, his office and almost in an airplane. This time it was so-so. I attribute that to the brash pinkish light that makes my skin look very white and distracted me. He kept his eyes shut while making love, which led me to believe that he was fantasizing about doing it with someone else, and that made things worse. Somehow we managed to climax. But we were both conscious of inaugurating a new and unaccustomed shelter of love even though it was only a rented and badly furnished apartment. We both seemed to feel better when the walls turned bluish and the light began to fade. He moved his thin, soft body across the room to the bath. I heard him whistling between his teeth and arose too. Almost immediately I felt his hand on my buttocks, then between my legs and went limp. I don't know how on earth he manages to caress a woman without ever altering his facial expression. On the surface it all seemed like a performance of a real pro, a ladykiller, but maybe it was just a part of our love cycle, second round. At the beginning he used to be moved to tears and one could have thought that he even suffered being in love. Yes, love used to be a very serious business for him, and he looked at me with a disarming, disturbing intensity. He made a vow of love, we read together, walked hand in hand silently and filled with emotion through the remotest corners of the city; it all used to be so soothingly pleasant. It was still pleasant, and we would have made love once more, time permitting, but I saw him getting dressed and turning towards the window that gave onto the street. That is where his house was, his real one, without nylon covers or ashtrays in the shape of a toilet seat. Yes, his real home. When we had discussed getting the apartment I told him that it was absurdly close to his house, in fact just around the corner. I had thought that such an argument would have convinced him, but no.

"It's not a matter of distance, darling," he explained.

I tried to convince him that in spite of displaying a lot of *sang froid* the situation was clearly out of the ordinary. But at the same time it occurred to me that he could just as easily have told me that our love was very unusual too.

"But just a block away from your house," I kept on protesting. Yet, it really was not a matter of the distance. Did I actually believe that the graveness of the situation diminished with the distance we put between us and his home? With that kind of a criterion we ought to be making love in the hallway that led to the swimming pool. (I know the lay-out of his house, where the furniture and books are placed and where he sleeps. In fact, I often imagined him at home. I know that while we were making love his wife would be working on a ceramic vase or some other craft.) I still kept on shaking my head but without much determination because arguing with him always brought me to the brink of a desperate feeling, a feeling of losing everything, even a part of that grand total that was enough to keep me going, full of anxiety, of weakening whenever a showdown cast its shadow between us. So I answered: "All right, let's get the apartment."

So he gave me the keys, and then came the plastic flowers and the love-making in that bizarre light and almost in view of his real home. Later I pointed a finger at that house and vainly tried to arouse his conscience. He seemed to suffer from a case of moral anesthesia; and there I was, lying on my belly while his fingers were gliding over my naked buttocks, looking straight at the green façade done in a sort of dubious style. I could see his garage door, the driveway, the front door, the second-story window giving onto a balcony, the stone work. I could imagine him entering and leaving as if I were watching him through a gun sight. Bang, bang, he would fall towards the right in front of the door, his youthful head perforated by the bullet as I would be gazing through the gun sight from the window in apartment 604, just as it happened to Kennedy, only there would not be a parade, CIA agents or a Secret Service man to throw himself on Jacqui: just the two of us, as it happens in a mad love story, and the woman pointing at the man caught in the gun sight. I could easily do it right from this window but I also knew that it would never happen. So I turned to look at him again and took in his lax and peaceful body and his beautiful penis, stilled by the cold water; and then I once more met his stare that showed neither lover nor hatred, only sadness. I tried to guess if the view of the green house from the window depressed him, but there was no way to know anything. He put on his beige shirt and knotted his tie. Seated on the bench he carefully combed his unruly black hair. I remember sitting at the edge of the bed, naked and unnerved, without strength. Then he started to caress me again and we ended up the way he foresaw it: everything seemed so natural and yet so painful. Our daily dose of sin—if there was such a thing—would amount to the same right across the street from his home as on top of the Andes. A distance of ten thousand miles would not change the nature of our doings.

The following visits went much better, and I began to establish a daily routine. I ate breakfast in an elegant bar that would soon be out of business because I was their only customer. They very respectfully called me madame, and I just sat there sipping my coffee. I expected him somewhere around lunch time; he usually called first. Sometimes, upon hearing my voice, he broke into laughter. At one time the sound of the happy laughter had gotten my hopes up, but that is over. My role had been defined very clearly and then tied in neatly with the apartment that was a short block away from his home: the bedroom, the bathroom and the kitchen now demanded more of me than any earlier memories tied to both of us. You are a part of us now since you live here, they seemed to whisper to me. And he said the same thing one day. So I began to belong; and the janitor started to greet me jovially, and I met a somewhat older woman neighbor, less hostile than the other ones on my floor that were all kept by somebody too.

I tried to improve the looks of the apartment. Although I refrained from throwing out the plastic monstrosities the place began to look better as time went on. I even stopped noticing the camp. Finally I took off the nylon covers from the couch where we both spent so much time exciting each other to the point of exasperation. I changed the chairs around and bought a terrine.

Every day I purchased flowers from the same deferential indian woman and tried to get him used to seeing the roses. I don't know if he ever noticed them, but they represented a parallel to his appearance in my life: they bloomed and died. One day, lying on the bed he exclaimed: look at your roses. Seated by the bedroom window, I soon learned about his routine comings and goings. The car in the driveway meant: at home. The car parked on the street meant: possibility. The car gone: absence. When he came to see me he left the car on an avenue that crosses his street diagonally. The car could have become a problem, but nothing ever happened and no one ever saw us together. Every weekend I went through the same elaborate torture. Actually it started Fridays because in Lima people have the perverse custom of taking care of their social life that lasted through Sunday. After a while I also found myself involved socially during those two and half days which at first used to drive me crazy. I tried to meet people, made friends, prepared dinners and got to know other solitary beings like myself. Sometimes a pair of blissful lovers came over. It probably made them feel good to be faced with a lonely woman like me, the antithesis of happiness and fulfillment. And so I tried very hard to stay busy Friday evenings, the endless Saturdays and the sleepy, sunny Sundays. I sunbathed and drank like a cossack. By Sunday morning my eyes hurt, my eyelids were swollen and I just wanted to die lying there in bed. Then I began to hear the melody of a song, the insistent barking of a dog, the cooing of a turtle dove nearby, then street noises, a car honking. Thus I knew the weekend had arrived and he would play his assigned role of a dutiful husband and father. Later I saw him coming down the steps to the car dressed in a blue zipped-up jacket and sort of leaning against the wind. I hoped that he might look up to my window, but of course he did no such thing. Try ESP I said to myself, anything, just so long as he would look over here, think of me, find me, be aware that I was watching him. He never did. Once his children appeared. I saw a boy, about eight, and he had the same head, the same nose. To tell the truth, nobody can distinguish a nose from a block's distance, but I could have sworn that I was seeing his father's head, his nose. There were altogether four children appearing and disappearing over there, but it was the one with the identical nose who made me feel sick. I believe that a woman can manage to give up a man but almost never the son that could have been. I still felt ill when reaching for the whisky bottle and receiving the umpteenth invitation for the day: I could lunch at Status, go to the movies in Pacifico or have tea at La Sueca with Mariana who by the way had been his mistress. To see Mariana was quite an experience because her disillusionment and sense of failure were extremely conducive to put me on guard. It was like telling myself: watch out or you will wind up the same way. Of course Mariana had never lived in a campy apartment within shouting distance of his home; that was a privilege I fiercely claimed for myself. But Mariana functioned as a kind of alarm bell and I returned to my seat with a sort of desperate need to look at him again. I could not make up my mind whether I should consider myself lucky or cursed. All I discovered was that Saturday turned out to be a more taxing day than Sunday since on Sunday I could look forward to Monday morning and his voice over the telephone.

I think we were both expecting things to come to a halt, but no. It was so beautiful to open the door, hesitate a little, gaze at his slender body, the eyes I loved so much, the unruly hair and the face that remained unsmiling before, during and after the marvellous kisses. Sometimes we had an outing at the ocean where the coast feels dry and sandy. Or we would go to Barranco Square to look at the statue of the naked woman who was washing her hands. One might think that we lived like condemned people, but that was not true; we experienced unique ways of being and observed little gestures that made us see life the way it could have been. There was the way in which he leafed through books running his fingers over the covers, his determination to reject the German philosophers, his lack of interest in my writings, and his coat slung carelessly over a chair. All of this held an enormous attraction for me. At the beauty shop the girl called Ruth gave me a camp hairdo that matched the apartment. He seldom noticed hairdos but I felt a fascination in waiting for him in my camp coiffure and being aware of the moment and the place we would share. Soon I realized that I actually liked living like this more than any other way I had experienced until now and, what was worse, that I would never get over it. One might think that he would have shown a similar reaction but he did not. He came and went smoothly, without showing an effort or a hesitation: so many hours at work, so many at home, so many in my apartment. He really did not spend much time with me: about three hours, sometimes more, sometimes less. We slept close to each other, and from that time on I knew that sleep is conducive to communion. The bed became impregnated with our body odors.

One lonely Saturday, however, it kept on raining. I saw him coming and going from my window, loading children into the station wagon and opening the car door for wifey. From a distance one acquires a certain perspective; for instance, I found out that most of my waking hours were spent in utter boredom while he showed me his constant obligation to his family. I also discovered that I only became alive in his presence and that nothing would ever change as long as he would return to me. But I began to visualize my existence without his presence and diagnosed the consequences: exhaustion, anomie and spiritual death.

In the meantime, he had settled wifey in her seat and quieted down the children. I lost track of the time and when I looked again the car had returned and wifey had disappeared inside, but I had a good look at the children, especially the boy with his father's nose and a thin girl that wore his sad face. I watched him climbing up the steps, carrying grocery bags, come back outside and carrying three boxes into the house. I looked at him as if he were an insect placed under a magnifying glass that depicted him very neatly and clearly, like a colored photo. This rainy Saturday without him broke something inside of me and I thought of the several invitations to go somewhere. What made me feel worse was that kid with the funny nose, that diabolical and yet innocent duplicate of himself. Some day that child would witness his death.

The bad part started on Monday when he returned and his kisses felt as intoxicating as ever. For a while I thought that hearts and magnifying glasses could be altered somehow, but of course that did not happen. I might as well have expected him to see how wrong the whole situation was. So in spite of this very promising Monday I waited anxiously for the weekend and no longer looked out of the window. I just imagined him loading up the car with wifey and the kids, and my insides tore up again. Better that way, my love, I said to myself as I grabbed my suitcase. Maybe I should have reconsidered everything but somehow I could not do it. Looking out of the window I saw him park the car on the driveway and for the last time took in his thin body, that purveyor of so much physical pleasure. Then I picked up a couple of personal belongings, returned the monstrosities to their rightful place, locked the front door from the outside and never saw that beloved man again.

AMALIA JAMILIS

Amalia Jamilis was born in 1936 in La Plata, the provincial capital not far from Buenos Aires. She studied art at the University of Buenos Aires. For a number of years she lived in the city and published her collections of short stories. A few years ago she moved to the isolated seaport of Bahia Blanca in the south of the giant province of Buenos Aires, where she lives with her two daughters and teaches art and visual education at the local Art Institute.

Between 1967 and 1971 she published three volumes of short stories that brought her national recognition. *Detrás de las columnas* (1967) received the Pen Club prize; *Los días sin suerte* (1969) won first prize in a national short story contest held in Mar del Plata, and the Emecé Publishers first prize in 1969.

Amalia Jamilis gives the impression of being a very introverted and gentle person who is perhaps afraid of challenging the awesome and complex manifestations of life. In this she seems to parallel the expression and existence of her characters. Jamalis's characters go about their daily business, be it shop-lifting or prostitution, without blaming the social forces and human factors that have contributed to their "downfall." Her female protagonists suffer legal retributions and self-righteous rejection with amazing equinimity; in fact, they never cease to reach out for a meaningful human relationship in spite of the vast and overpowering urban indifference, alienation and hostility that surrounds them. They somehow manage to draw on their own candor and vulnerability to find the human

101

102

element in their antagonists. If failure reveals human nature to a much larger degree than success, the prostitute in "Night Shift" as well as the female shoplifter and the soft-hearted detective in "Department Store" belong to that special category of losers, admirable in their vulnerability and only-too-human defects.

BIBLIOGRAPHY

Detrás de las columnas, 1967 (stories)
Los días sin suerte, 1969 (stories)
Los trabajos nocturnos, 1971 (stories)

Night Shift

Amalia Jamilis

Half way between the sidewalk and the car I felt already sorry that I had accepted. He pushed the car door open and I thanked him as I slid inside, but then I gave him a good once-over because there was something about the guy I disliked.

"What's your name," he asked and tried to smile.

"Olimpia," I told him.

"That's such a matronly name," he commented while watching the ten o'clock traffic that was still heavy. "But you seem to be a very pretty girl, even delicate."

I can't really say what made me dislike this guy. He drove quite carefully, used the brakes a lot and veered to the left and the right always watching the other cars. He kept on talking and from time to time managed to look at me giving me the impression that I was irresistible.

Then he said, "Why are you wearing this kind of a dress?"

I had an outfit on that was handpainted by Cela. I wasn't really crazy about it myself, but Cela had explained to me that he had drawn some Indian gods all in black and white. On the street people stared at it and some boys even laughed and made an obscene joke because the design featured a figure right between my breasts. Anyhow, the dress was a gift and when I wore it I felt as if all my friends from home were close to me. But I couldn't begin to tell all this to the guy, so I just answered:

"It's a gift from a friend."

He didn't say anything, but at the next traffic light he looked at me for a long time and smiled kind of sadly.

On Cordoba Avenue the shop windows shone softly in pink and light blue colors, the traffic had thinned out and I looked at the trees thinking all along that he was going to take me to a hotel near the port. So I told him, "I know a good hotel in Almagro, the Excelsior."

103

But he just shrugged his shoulders and replied: "You must be kidding, that's clear on the other side of town. There are some good joints close by, there's the Eros and they serve champagne there. You like that?"

"No," I said, "I don't think I know the Eros. I've never been at that place."

"I mean the champagne," he explained.

"Oh yes, the champagne," I answered, "sure, I like it a lot. It sort of tickles me and then I feel like laughing and singing."

"You like to sing?" he kept on asking.

"Yes," I told him, "in the Arizona Bar they asked me to sing *Tres palabres* and *Nosotros.*"

"Nosotros?" He found that strange. "What a name for a song?"

"Sure," I told him, "Gregorio Barrios sang it. It goes: We who love each other so, we must say goodbye, don't ask another word."

"Pretty stupid lyrics, if you ask me," he said and put on the brakes.

That made me pretty mad. In the first place, the song is beautiful and romantic, just the way I like songs; and secondly this character was carrying on as if he owned the world.

"Just then he said, "Open the door, this is the Eros."

We got out of the car. The Eros impressed me although it lacked a grand entrance and a couple of letters were burned out in the marquee. In the lobby we passed an endless sofa and came upon a Christmas tree adorned with beads and snowflakes.

Seeing our surprise the manager explained that because of the coming holidays they had put up the tree and loaded it down with shiny balls, colored icicles, little angels and clusters of mint and mistletoe.

The crowd at the Eros loved all of that, probably because it gave them a homey feeling. Too bad that all the rooms were taken; in fact, we saw a number of couples waiting around in the hallway.

I kept on looking at the Christmas tree. Underneath it they had placed pine branches on green paper; it looked just like the woods. I got all excited and called the guy: "Come here and look at this, dear, the lights go on and off."

He came over to me and said: "Don't call me *dear*, don't ever call me that."

I looked at him. "But what, why . . . ," I began.

"Well," he hesitated, "you could call me . . . maybe . . . Rodolfo. Yeah, Rodolfo. That has a beautiful tragic ring: Rodolfo Valentino, Rodolfo of Hapsburg."

"What's that?" I stammered, but by that time we were on our way out. We climbed into the car and took off in the direction of downtown.

"The Excelsior is really a fine hotel," I reminded him. I was beginning to feel a little tired and impatient. I started to think about the Pampa, Tierno, Cela and the kids that were probably still out playing on the patio.

"Let's try our luck at the Royal," he said curtly. "Same thing every Saturday. No vacancies anywhere."

On Paraguay Street near Lavalle Square somebody waved at us from a car window. Rodolfo shouted, "It's Buby. Of all places."

We stopped. Two men and three or four girls jumped out of the other car. They all patted Rodolfo on the shoulders and laughed real loud. Then they started to talk in another language, English I guess.

I stayed behind in the car and felt like crying. Around me couples were walking hand in hand. Some people were eating ice cream. A couple was taking a dog for a walk.

Every so often voices and laughter floated over to me from the other car. After some fifteen minutes Rodolfo broke away from the group carrying a small package.

"I thought it was Buby," he said leaving the package on the back seat, "but it was his brother. They look alike. Never met him before, didn't even know Buby had a brother. He asked me to take this package to Arenales Street. I owe Buby lots of favors so we better get going."

When we got to Arenales, Rodolfo said that there were no parking spaces so he would drive around the block until I had delivered the package. I got out and looked for the right number. It turned out to be a bar called La Cabaña. Inside I could barely make out two dim red lights. Somebody close asked: "You have your ticket?"

"No," I said.

"Well, if you don't have a ticket, you can't come in," the voice went on.

"But I have to come in, there is this package I have to deliver," I started to explain.

"Sorry," the voice continued, "I can't let you in."

By now my eyes had gotten used to the darkness and I could make out a short, fat man in an expensive tux with two red stripes instead of a tie. His head was covered with gaudy curls that gave him a gay look.

"But," I stammered, "Buby's brother gave us this package . . . "

"Cut it out, girlie," the little man shut me up, "everybody has ants in their pants tonight. I'll have to get Betolé."

"But the package," I insisted.

"If Betolé finds out about this all hell will break loose," he kept on.

He was standing behind some kind of counter. In the background I could make out some elegant clothes hanging in a closet. Suddenly a deafening noise broke out. From somewhere inside about a dozen people rushed towards us, shouting, singing, clicking glasses.

"Now there is a real gal for you," said a very thin, tall man with a round beard, "maybe it is Jake Arancibia. He dresses up as a hooker once in a while."

"The package," I said softly. A hand appeared from somewhere and grabbed it.

"Buby's brother sends it," I said in a firmer voice.

"Buby's brother, Buby's brother," echoed the crowd.

"And here comes Betolé," said the little man looking at me with venom.

"Who let her in?" asked a very fat and white woman coming up to me. "You were not supposed to let anybody in without a ticket."

"Well," I said, a little relieved, "I'm leaving, so good night."

Getting rid of that package made me feel better, but several voices were shouting: "No, never. She's a real hooker, she has to stay. Betolé, don't you let her go."

I stared at the fat woman. Her whiteness seemed to shine between the two red lights. She wore a long, silvery dress, similar to a tunic. Her sandals revealed two absurdly small feet whose nails were painted in a darkish red.

A glass of champagne appeared out of nowhere and Betolé held it up to me. "Here you are, dear, sip it slowly or you might get tipsy."

"But I don't want to," I said. I was afraid and felt like screaming. Somebody pushed the glass against my mouth and made my lip bleed. The blood began to trickle down to my chin.

"That brings good luck," shouted the man with the beard, and everybody dipped their finger in my blood.

Several of them started to carry me off to a smoke-filled room. The deafening music from a record player covered up the shouting, the laughter and the tinkling of the glasses. They left me standing on top of a table and the little man with the curls screamed: "Now I'm going to give it to you good."

He unzipped his pants and I began to sob and shake all over.

"Don't be a show-off, Esteban," said Betolé calmly, "you know you can't do anything. Just stop it, Esteban."

Everyone kept on shouting and drinking. Some, like the guy with the beard, began to dance and go into contortions.

Suddenly Rodolfo's head popped up. He looked baffled and was threatening the little man in curls with his fists. Now he became the center of attention. Three or four people surrounded him, some pushed him from behind, others grabbed his lapels. The man with the beard had stopped dancing. Although he was terribly skinny his hands worked like a vise as he kept Rodolfo's hands pinned behind his back. The little man in curls filled a glass and was about to throw it into Rodolfo's face when Betolé intervened. She simply raised a hand and said: "Enough, let them go."

She really seemed to be the boss around there because they let us go and we beat it outside.

Rodolfo's shirt was hanging out and his jacket was torn. Someone had hit him because he sported a shiner on his cheek. My lip was still bleeding and my clothes looked wrinkled and dirty. People on the street were staring at us and laughing.

"Poor Olimpia," said Rodolfo looking at me, "let's hit the Royal now, take a good bath and drink some whisky. This was awful."

"Horrible," I said.

I turned around and looked at La Cabaña just as someone was throwing Buby's package into the street. I told Rodolfo and we quickly crossed to pick it up and then went to the car.

"At least we might take a peek at what's inside that precious package," I said as the car moved along on Juncal Street.

"Not on your life," he answered, "I owe Buby a lot of favors."

"So what?" I replied, but he didn't even bother to answer. He parked opposite a hotel with stairs that had a wooden bannister. It looked like some old mansion that had seen better days, quiet and dark like the night. A big neon sign flashed *Royal Hotel.* The neon light hit the leaves of the sycamore trees.

Inside we faced a huge counter with a zinc cover. Almost hidden in shadows stood several archways whose gypsum pillars were carved in the shape of naked women.

While Rodolfo asked for a room I just stared at the fluorescent lights and began to feel immensely sad and tired. The clerk led us to a large salon furnished with easy chairs, sofas, a false fire place with red bricks and a star-shaped clock. Rodolfo put his arm around my waist and asked: "Like it?"

"Yes," I answered, although I wasn't sure what he was referring to.

Just about then a man in striped pyjamas and worn-out house shoes came in. "Say, mister," he said to Rodolfo, "you'd better watch out for your car."

"What's that?" asked Rodolfo letting go of me. I noticed that his face was turning red all over.

"I saw you two get out of the car," the man went on. "I was out getting a breath of fresh air when I saw those two characters walking up to your car and trying the doors. Since they were locked they tried the trunk and made off with a package."

"The package," cried Rodolfo and began to run to the exit. I followed him. We ran between the sycamores and cinnamon trees on the silent street filled with a strong scent of jasmin. Rodolfo was swearing out loud. At the intersection he hesitated and looked in several directions, but we could only make out the blueish outline of houses and the shadow of the trees under the street lights.

Suddenly the silence was shattered by shouts, sirens and people running.

"The cops," murmured Rodolfo staring at some men running straight towards us. "And me without papers," he moaned. "I just didn't know what I was doing earlier, must have been drunk." Then he gave me an address in Belgrano and told me to hurry there and notify his brother the lawyer.

Belgrano is awfully far from downtown. But I returned to the Royal and asked the clerk to call for a taxi. After I told him what happened he looked at me with pity and said that he thought Rodolfo would be on his way to the police station by now but he would help me out because he knew someone there.

"The taxi came and I was off. At night the huge city was reduced to an endless series of darkish streets hiding their shops, restaurants, bookstores and grocery marts. We stopped in a deserted street that seemed to belong right in the countryside. But the houses looked impressive: wrought-iron gates, white archways and tall pillars. Rodolfo's house was surrounded by a high green fence. Just then I realized that I had no money on me. The driver was looking at me in the rear-view mirror. So I told him: "I'm without a penny, but I'll leave you my ring." I took it off. The rhinestones looked pretty good in the dark. The driver suddenly smiled and rejected my offer. "Why don't you go inside first and see if someone will lend you the money."

I felt really grateful but for some reason his face hardened again. I put my ring back on and got out. The iron gate stood half open. I walked along a row of tiles looking at the windows, afraid they would take me for a thief. At the huge wooden door I had to knock a number of times until a servant opened up and looked at me with sleepy eyes and an irritated expression.

"The cops got Rodolfo," I told him.

For a while he looked at me with surprise; then he burst out laughing.

"Well, that's okay, sweetheart, Rodolfo doesn't live here, but maybe you and I can have some fun together."

A feeling of helplessness surged all over me. At the same time I remembered that Rodolfo was a name he had made up in front of that Christmas tree at the Eros.

"I don't know his real name," I shouted desperately. "He's in jail and wants his brother to get him out. He's a lawyer, isn't he?"

The servant's face became serious. "Yes, he's an attorney, but he isn't here, and when these two go out anything can happen."

"Well, what do I do now?" I asked.

"I don't know," he said, "let them be; they are always getting into trouble. They are old enough to look out for themselves."

He closed the door in my face and I slowly went to the gate. Then I realized that I forgot to get Rodolfo's papers. So I turned around and walked back expecting that servant to be madder than hell for being bothered again. But from one of the upper windows a girl motioned me to come to the side door. When she opened up I noticed that she looked very young and friendly. She couldn't have been more than fifteen or sixteen; apparently she was a maid. Her face seemed honest and kind, very much the country girl with dark, tired eyes that shone quietly.

We went into the kitchen where she prepared coffee for the two of us. While I was sipping from the cup I began to tell her all about this crazy night: the Christmas tree at the Eros, the little bastard with his curls and that fat Betolé woman. She took me to the bathroom to fix myself up a bit, and then she went to get Rodolfo's papers, only his name was José Maria Campodónico.

I looked into the mirror. The cut on my lip and the dried-up blood gave me a forlorn look. My hair was hanging down in wet streaks sticking to my face and neck. That was enough to make me take off my clothes, open the faucets of the bath tub and sprinkle the water with bathing salt and cologne. I spent a long time just soaking, forgetting all about Rodolfo and everything else. She finally returned with the papers and watched while I dried myself and applied some talcum powder. She didn't care.

"You look like a new woman," she said and offered to iron my dress, but suddenly I remembered Rodolfo, the waiting taxi driver and the money. I told her and she got her purse and handed me several hundred peso bills.

I straightened out my dress and ran outside. The taxi was gone. The street lay there, quiet. The wind made the leaves tremble and the moths made a sort of cold noise hitting against the street lights.

I walked a lot of blocks before finding another taxi, but I felt fresh and rested as if I had slept all night.

The clerk at the Royal seemed happy to see me. He said, "Now let's find out if your friend is at the local precinct," and dialed a number. Sure enough, that's where they had Rodolfo.

So I went to the police station walking along the sycamore trees and the houses with their windows open while the wind blew a humid air in my face announcing a thunderstorm.

I found Rodolfo in a bare room sitting on a long bench, dishevelled and breathing hard, his shirt tails still hanging out.

"I gave your papers to the desk sergeant," I said, getting close to him. "They'll let you go now."

He slowly glanced at me with a far-away look in his deep-set eyes. I noticed now that his nose looked big and sad and that his mouth sagged with an impotent gesture.

"It doesn't matter now," he answered with a strangled voice as if he was about to cry.

"What do you mean, it doesn't matter? What about the hotel and the package?" I shouted, angry at his dejection and suddenly feeling that I had reached my limit. I came closer and looked him squarely in the eye. My stare must have shown a mixture of ardor and anxiety. He lowered his head.

"The hotel?" he repeated mechanically. "I feel awfully tired, I couldn't do anything now. I think it's best that you go now, we can get together another time."

"And the package?" I asked.

"Oh, that. A while ago I suddenly remembered that Buby and I both got out from doing military service. I drew a low number and Buby was the only son of a widow."

I stopped listening, slowly turned around, went out into the street and started to walk, taking my time.

After three or four blocks, a car stopped next to me. A man leaned out of the window and invited me in. While I closed the door I thought that this was a real classy car and this way I might still make up for a lost night.

Department Store

Amalia Jamilis

What a coincidence to run into the guy with the brown suit, the one from the Department Store, just as I was going over to Gilda's. What can you do; it's a small world and you never know how something is going to turn out. Because I met Gilda thanks to this guy.

If I tell you the story you won't believe it. In those days I used to hang around that Dago gal. She got busted working the shops between Liniers and Flores uptown. After a month at the Good Shepherd jail for women she came to see me. Well, we got to talking and I finally told her that she might as well try the big Department Stores downtown because there was enough for everybody. Later I came across her a number of times. She must have been doing all right because she was all dolled up, gloves and everything, just like a lady.

I took my time casing the big Department Stores, checking the rush hours and the slack periods. That dumb Dago never paid any attention to the preliminaries and that's why she got busted all the time. The nuns at the Good Shepherd already waited for her to come back so they could teach her how to crochet rugs. That Dago is really something else.

Well, the afternoon in question the store was packed because they had a big sale. I squeezed between two counters with a big pile of dark blouses. Half looking I grabbed a handful and tucked them in my bag. Next to me stood a kid who kept saying he wanted to go back to Grimoldi's because there they had toys. I was about to bag a few pairs of men's socks when I hear that kid yelling to his mother: "She stole those things from the counter, she did." His mother told him that he was mistaken and that the salesgirls are there to watch out for things like that, but that damned kid kept on yelling that he saw me stealing the blouses and I wanted to do a disappearing act. Actually I felt like belting that snot-nose one, but he just wouldn't shut his trap and people began to gather around us.

112

That's when this fatty blond guy with glasses and a brand-new suit hurried over. He must have been some sort of manager and all the salesgirls practically curtsied and called him Mr. Burton and telling him about what the kid had said. This Burton guy looked me over and I thought that he was going to let me have it right there and then, but he just edged me past the crowd to a little private office with nothing in it but two chairs. All along this guy mumbled "Let's see now, let's see now," and pushed a button on the wall. After a few seconds a guy in a brown suit and a sad face came in. Suddenly the Englishman grabbed my bag and let the blouses tumble onto the floor.

"Always this happens during sales," he said in his funny Spanish, looking straight at the other man, "too much to handle today."

"Yes, Mr. Burton," answered the guy in the brown suit.

"Now you stay here while I go and call the police precinct."

Only then did I realize how angry this Burton really was. This all-business coldness of his made shivers run down my spine, I swear. The guy in brown just kept on saying, "Yes, Mr. Burton," but he looked as if he was thinking about something else. When this Mr. Burton left the room I asked him straight out: "And now what's going to happen?" I don't know why I said that because I really knew the answer and thought I'd end up like the Dago, but he didn't answer me right away. He fished a cigarette out of his pocket and started to blow the smoke up to the ceiling. Then I saw that his brown suit was double-breasted, with too many buttons and shiny all over. I was sure that his wife must have brushed and ironed it all the time but she still couldn't get the shine and the wrinkles out. His face went with his suit, sort of tired and ordinary. He wore his hair long and it fell down on his forehead and at the temples, and that reminded me a little of Ledesma, remember him? He's probably graduated by now and all that, just think how time flies. Well, anyhow, this guy in the brown suit kept on smoking and staring at his toes. Through the glass door I could see Burton on the phone. In a few minutes the cops are going to show and the jig will be up, I thought. Suddenly the guy looked straight at me.

"If you've got the guts to jump out of the window you'll find yourself on a high-rise patio that leads to the back of the block. Then you'll be on your own," he said.

I didn't trust my ears. "The window?" I asked in a stupid sort of voice. In the next room the Englishman was still gesticulating and yelling into the phone.

"The window," repeated the guy in brown, "either it's that way or the other. It really matters little, they're all the wrong ways."

That's when I started to get real scared because I began to realize that the poor sap was nutty, and you never know what a nut is going to do. Just remember what happened with that painter fellow from the Modern Art Institute.

"If you want to get away, better beat it right now before Mr. Burton comes back," said the guy in brown. I felt like thanking him or leaving my phone number at the boarding house, but I'm not much on ceremony and besides I was in a hell of a hurry. When I opened the window I thought that the noise would alert that damned Englishman, but nothing happened. I looked back and saw the guy in brown staring at the wall and his face looked as if someone had just socked it to him; he even seemed to be talking out loud to himself. I tell you, I almost cried seeing a man going off the deep end like that. From the window I made it to a narrow passage way that ended up at a staircase that led to a terrace where the sun was melting the tar-paper floor. By now the damned Englishman would be screaming at that poor guy all on account of me. Well, from the terrace it was easy to jump down onto this patio and then I found some stairs belonging to an apartment building.

My heart about stopped beating when I ran into Gilda. Up to now everything had been easy as pie and here I find this woman polishing the brass on the railing. Later this Gilda told me that she never forgets a face—something all these janitors have in common—and that at the time she suddenly got suspicious about me, but I just pulled up my stockings while she stared at me.

"This just isn't my day," I told her, "I get into the wrong building and now I'm beginning to feel sick to my stomach."

Well, that broke the ice and she led me to her room and fixed me a cup of tea right there and then. Later we became real close and I went to see her often and we had tea and talked and I told her about my living with Ledesma near the hospital and about Frenchie, but I never mentioned the Department Store caper.

And now, all of a sudden I ran into the guy with the brown suit. Isn't life a scream?

I was walking along Libertad Street when he saw me. He lowered his head as if trying to tell me that it had been all his fault. I'm sure that he thought I was going to play it cool and keep on walking because when I stopped in front of him he gave me a look that made me feel worse than when that damned kid started yelling in the Department Store.

"They fired me that very day," he finally said with a tired voice and he looked as if he had been walking around all day.

"Sure," I said.

"Mr. Burton accused me of letting you go on purpose."

"Sure," I repeated.

"But the whole mess was my fault, not yours."

"Sure, sure, sure," I said while my hand touched his face, combed through his hair and got stuck on the shirt button. When I unbuttoned his shirt the bypassers looked at us and laughed, and that's when I grabbed him by his arm and we started to run like crazy because the 102 minibus that stops one block away from my boarding house had just reached the corner. I knew that I owed him for that Department Store deal and I had to pay him back the only way I knew how.

EUGENIA CALNY

Eugenia Calny was born in the far-away province of San Juan in Argentina in 1937. Like so many woman writers, Calny started her literary career in journalism, particularly magazine writing; in her case, women's publications. After a number of her short stories had appeared in different Argentine magazines, they were collected in a volume entitled *El agua y la sed* in 1960.

Seven years later her second book of stories came out with the title *Las mujeres virtuosas.* In this book the majority of the stories feature female protagonists who attempt to overcome the determinism of their environment as they face incomprehension, isolation and even open hostility. Calny often establishes an open clash between psychological and social forces, a technique she also applied to her novel *Clara al amanecer* (1972), a runner-up in the Paidos Publishing House contest.

In 1978 she returned to the short story form with a volume called *La tarde de los ocres dorados.* Here love, time and solitude are the main elements that pervade the destinies of most of her heroines, creating a sort of magical trinity in the process. In the story selected for this anthology, "Siesta," the main character faces these elements as she mocks herself in a rather wistful manner, only too aware of her futile attempts to transcend her hopeless condition as an aging, penniless and lonely woman in a tenement house who still dares to dream about youth and love.

117

BIBLIOGRAPHY

El agua y la sed, 1960 (stories)
Las mujeres virtuosas, 1967 (stories)
Clara al amanecer, 1972 (novel)
La tarde de los ocres dorados, 1978 (stories)

Siesta

Eugenia Calny

The young man got out of the pre-war Ford in his wash-and-wear summer suit carrying a briefcase and wiping the February sweat from his forehead during the siesta hour.

"He is too good-looking," Isabel decided while spying through the crochet curtain. "He ought to be starring in soap operas. Poor guy, he has got a case of work ethics and really wants to sell something."

She smiled when she saw him checking the address in his little appointment book.

"He is not sure that anybody in a place like this could possible be a customer." Isabel smiled when she saw him asking the washer woman's son. "In five minutes the whole tenement house will know about this."

Some children were trying to climb on the old Ford like giant clumsy flies and he tried to scare them away . . .

There was a timid knock. Isabel opened the door looking him straight in the eye. Deep inside and somehow far away something made her tremble.

"Miss Isabel Linares?"

She nodded looking down at ther transparent blouse that showed the symmetrical outline of her bra. The nylon material was sticking to her back and felt wet under her arm pits.

"I represent Asbasian Brothers, Airconditioning."

He reminded her of the favorite book she had at her bedside as a girl: *The Sheik.* She tried a little smile baring a gold tooth, her only jewel.

She was remembering her old girl friend Felisa fantasizing: "As far as I'm concerned if a man looks like the Sheik, he can kidnap me any time." Puppy love: the Sheik, Becquer's poem about the swallows, the *Nocturne* by Acuña, Nervo's and Dario's verses . . .

119

"I am the technical advisor . . . maybe it slipped your mind, but you made an appointment for three o'clock to see me today."

She became serious. "But without obligations."

"Of course, no obligation to buy." His body seemed to sway in the early afternoon heat.

"Please, sit down. I'll fix you something cool."

He literally dropped into the chair. She brought him a tall glass of coca cola with ice. He drained it in one gulp with a childlike, greedy expression.

"Thanks. This feels like paradise."

"Maybe more like purgatory." Well, all right. They seemed to get along fine. She felt like confiding a little in him, going back to old times.

" . . . in those days we had no New Wave, no strip tease, no crazy dances, no television, no round-table discussions about complexes and traumas . . . "

"Nor did we have electric mixers, washing machines or air conditioners."

Isabel showed her disappointment. Good grief. Couldn't he stop acting like a salesman for just one minute?

He measured the room with his eyes: the bed without a headboard, the cage with the silent, white canary who was jumping around, the ancient radio, the old wardrobe with the oval mirror and the table featuring a red formica top, the only "modern" piece of furniture in the place.

She felt a certain pleasure looking at him and reading his thoughts. "Stupid woman. Making me lose my time like this and having me come in this heat. She must be nutty."

But his eyes shone with such a serenity framed by the longest eyelashes she had ever seen on a man. How many women would try to get their cheek close to his face just to feel the soft caress of these eyelashes? And after that? The thought made her feel dizzy.

"The airconditioner would be for this studio?"

Good for him, calling this dump a studio. He spread out his catalog.

"Why do you ask?" She felt a little defensive. "Wouldn't it work for this *studio*?"

"On the contrary. It is ideal. According to the measurements one horse power would be sufficient."

"And what about financing?" She was almost amused asking the question.

For a moment he looked straight at her. Then he pointed at the catalog and began to scribble on a piece of paper.

"There are three possibilities. A downpayment of nine thousand nine hundred and ninety pesos and monthly installments of five thousand pesos, which comes to a total with interest charges of course . . . "

While he busied himself with the figures (she hated arithmetic) she glanced at the open catalog. It was a colored picture entitled "The ideal condition for a happy home": the head of the family, good looks, greying hair, smoking his pipe and watching television; his wife, a red head dressed in the latest fashion, sitting next to him, busily knitting; on the shaggy, orange-colored rug two blond children, neat and well-fed, playing with blocks; a Siamese cat completed the happy scene.

" . . . naturally, by paying cash you would save a considerable amount."

"Sorry, that is out of the question," Isabel answered with a good deal of candor.

"I understand," he replied with a charming display of understanding.

"Are there several models?" Isabel inquired as she turned the pages of the catalog.

"Two. A cooling unit and one that also converts to a heater in winter time. Considering the advantages, the price difference is minimal."

"And all those buttons?" asked Isabel staring at the glossy photo depicting a modern office in which the air conditioner had supplied instant happiness to the manager, the male employees and the secretary with the long, stylish legs.

"A free manual comes with delivery. It is simple to operate, even a child can do it."

"There are no children." She did not know why she said that. She felt the desire to rest her thin, pale hand on that tan, smooth skin that promised unknown pleasures . . .

"And to install this thing? It is so big. I understand that you might have to break through the outside wall."

"Yes, that is true." He seemed depressed now. "But the technicians can do that in half a day. The air conditioner would harmonize with the room; it is very esthetic."

"Of course, esthetic," she replied wrily. "Hot and cold too."

"Sure, you can adjust it: very cold or medium cool; same with the heat. Lots of air circulation. A real discovery of modern technology!"

Isabel sighed. She looked at him again. Then she picked up the papers.

"I will have to think it over. It is much more expensive than I thought. Since you don't give out prices over the phone . . . "

"Our policy, sorry."

". . . one has to bother you people to come to the house."

"That's what we are here for. Service is our motto." The voice had taken on a somewhat sullen thickness.

So that is what you are here for. She looked again at his hands, his eyelashes, his tall figure. Under that polyester suit and the acetate shirt had to be a firm, browned skin, a wooly chest, a young body, as taut as a coiled spring.

"It is still so hot."

"Lucky I have my automobile."

He was closing his briefcase. Nice going. Calling this cave a studio and that relic an automobile. Maybe by now the kids had taken it apart.

"February can be hellish in Buenos Aires, right? When are you going on vacation?"

"I already went." He smiled guiltily. "In December."

"Oh. Mar del Plata?"

"No. San Clemente. It is quieter there." Then he added in a low voice: "It is also cheaper."

"Did you ever consider appearing in a TV series?"

He laughed. It was the most masculine sound she had heard in this room over the last ten years. Unless she wanted to count that one other time . . . but that man had been a nervous wreck, unhappy and impotent . . . Anyhow, she knew that outside the neighbors were listening. So much the better. It bothered her that he got up, ready to go, now that they had become something like old friends.

"Miss Linares, it has been a pleasure. Don't hesitate to call on me. My card. Salesman number seven."

So he was a number, like those prisoners at the concentration camp. A good number, though. Seven. There were the seven biblical years of famine and plenty. The seven years Boaz the shepherd waited for the hand of Ruth. The seven year itch with that gorgeous sexbomb whose life ended . . . But it had not been her fault. It must have been her husband, brainy, cold, insensitive to her suffering. No doubt he was the one who had pushed her into a nightmare of despair and death . . .

Isabel's eyes had become moist thinking about Marilyn Monroe's fate and the salesman was giving her a worried look. He left her two brochures: the one with the cat and the one with the happy, cool office. She walked him to the door. His lips seemed awfully dry, but it was too late to offer him another coke. Instead she scared away the kids by clapping her hands and yelling at them in a rather hoarse voice. They backed away.

"Where did you dig up this buggy, mister, from a museum?"

Isabel threatened the boy with her fist. The other kids roared with laughter. The salesman waved to her and walked over to his car with a careful air of dignity.

In her room the chairs looked so empty now. She touched the glass: it felt tepid. She did not quite know why the visit had left her feeling sad. She opened the little window and remembered that the air conditioner was to be installed in this wall. She remained a long time leaning against the window screen that was leaving its design on her forehead. She finally realized that one of the boys was making faces at her, but she felt too exhausted to even shout at him. After a while she dragged a chair onto the tenement patio and sat under the muscatel vine.

A few of the tenants were already in their chairs nearby. Some refused to greet her, she forgot what the reasons were. Others always tried to pry into her affairs. She did not really know why and did not care either. Some of them borrowed her kerosene stove and then invited her over to watch television.

"So, you had a visitor?" asked a fat, old woman who was drinking her mate tea while fanning herself with a piece of cardboard.

"Yes, a visitor. And your daughter?"

"Lying on the bed. Nausea all day long. Can't keep anything down."

"It is just those first months."

"That's what I say. Have to wait it out."

"And her husband?"

"He doesn't have nausea . . . " she giggled, "he has something wrong with his head."

The old woman kept on drinking her mate from the gourd. Isabel knew what would come next: the terrible inflation; the price of bread, meat, eggs and clothes going up every week. Just then the daughter came by. She looked exhausted, and her complexion matched the greenish housecoat that hung loosely around her haggard figure. Isabel was not about to witness an exchange of poisoned words between the two women and went to get the latest fashion magazine that she had borrowed from the beauty salon. The pregnant girl came and looked over Isabel's shoulder studying the glossy pictures.

"This coming winter boots are going to be in."

"Those cossack boots are nothing but a Russian plot," mumbled the mother. Just then a very old man came by. He walked unsteadily holding a bottle of cheap wine in each hand. He hit Isabel's stretched-out leg and made her lose a shoe.

"Damned old drunk," his wife shouted from somewhere nearby.

The old man excused himself and Isabel felt compelled to ask him about his son. The old man tried to laugh. Oh well, the boy was making progress. He had graduated from Reform School and entered prison. They caught him being the look-out for a gang that stole tires. The old man's eyes filled with tears. Now the local pimp walked by greeting Isabel very politely, his arm around the girl with the padded bra who worked in an Olivos nightclub that was raided once a week. The drunkard said: "If I only were twenty years younger, or even ten."

Isabel became fascinated by a colored picture that covered two pages: A shaggy carpet, white like a polar bear without a head. Mobile lamps. Fur-covered chairs with matching little pillows. Pink, yellow and cinnamon colors. Then a copper mural with an Egyptian motif. Little fawn-colored marble tables. Blue crystal grapes mounted on a wooden plate. Indoor plants. A combination bookshelf, bar and cabinet. In the background a folding door allowing a peek at the tempting yet chaste bedroom . . .

The drunkard's babbling came now from the common bathroom and blended in with his wife's loud complaints. Tinny pots rattled somewhere. A mildly obscene song floated through the air. A mattress creaked. One of the kids came running in crying and holding his bloodied nose. A young man with a bad leg carrying a can of paint and a brush went by whistling a song. The drunkard came out to meet him and told him why he could no longer work: he pulled up his pants legs and showed his varicose veins.

Isabel asked somebody for a pencil. Then, serene and relaxed, she wrote down a phone number and underlined *Free Housecalls by our expert sales personnel.*

LUISA VALENZUELA

As the daughter of Luisa Mercedes Levinson, Luisa Valenzuela was initiated at an early age into the world of the written word, working for magazines and practicing journalism. In 1958, when she was twenty, she left her native Buenos Aires to become the Paris correspondent for the Argentine daily *El Mundo*. There she also wrote programs for Radio Television Française and participated in the intellectual life of the then famous *Tel Quel* group and the structuralists.

Three years later she returned to Buenos Aires and joined Argentina's foremost newspaper, *La Nación*. In 1969 she came to the University of Iowa Writers Workshop on a Fulbright grant. In 1972 she obtained a scholarship to study pop culture and literature in New York. From then on she became an avid traveller, living in Spain, Mexico, New York and Buenos Aires, participating in conferences and continuing her journalism. All along she cultivated her fiction, begun at the age of fifteen.

Her first book, *Hay que sonreir* (1968) features Clara, a naïve country girl turned prostitute in Buenos Aires, whose adventures with a picaresque male world alternate between the humorous and the macabre. As the novel progresses, the anti-heroine's candor slowly changes into a pathetic stance under the constant attack of the city's anonymity, alienation and male rapacity. Her New York-Greenich Village experience resulted in *El gato eficaz* (1972), an experimental novel sustained largely by language and imagination.

But Luisa Valenzuela, like other Argentine women writers, cannot shut out her involvement with an Argentine society torn by violence, class struggle, dictatorship and dehumanization. Thus "Change of Guard" came into being. Written outside her native country, where it could not possibly be printed under the present regime, this unpublished long story epitomizes not only the struggle between individual freedom and despotism, but also the clash between the macho syndrome and female dignity.

BIBLIOGRAPHY

Hay que sonreir, 1966 (novel)
Los heréticos, 1967 (stories)
El gato eficaz, 1972 (novel)
Aqui pasan cosas raras, 1975 (novel)
"El que busca," 1980 (story)

Change of Guard

Luisa Valenzuela

The words

She is not at all surprised to be without a memory, to feel totally bereft of the past. Perhaps she fails to realize that life is an absolute nothing. But she is worried about something else: her ability to apply the proper name to each object and to receive a cup of tea when saying I want (and this "I want," this act of will, confuses her) when she says I want a cup of tea.

Martina waits on her hand and foot. She knows that name because Martina herself told her so and repeated it enough times for her to remember. As for herself, they told her that her name was Laura, but this name must belong to the clouded mystery that constitutes her present life.

Then there is the man: the one, he, hey, the one without a name whom she could call anything that came to mind because it worked, and the guy answered her even when she called him Hugo, Sebastian, Ignacio, Alfredo or whatever. And apparently he came often enough to quiet her down a little, putting a hand on her shoulder and adjacent areas in a sort of progression that held the promise of some tenderness.

And then there are the common objects: the ones called dishes, bath, book, bed, cup, table, door. What a feeling of despair, for instance, to face the so-called door without knowing what to do. A door locked with a key, to be sure, but the keys right there on the mantelpiece where she could reach them, and the lock easily to be undone, and the fascination of what lies beyond it, is something that she cannot face right now.

What was she, Laura or whatever her name was, doing on this side of that so-called door with its corresponding lock that was beckoning her to pass through? But she couldn't, not yet; sitting there facing that door, pondering and knowing that it was not to be, although apparently nobody really cared.

And suddenly that door opens and the one we shall now call Hector appears, proving that he too has his so-called keys that he'll use with a great ease. And looking carefully at his entrance—this has happened other times to the so-called Laura—she discovers that two other men arrived together with this Hector and remain on the outside of the door as if they meant to efface themselves. She calls them One and Two without ever really knowing who is who or whether it's always the same ones who come. But it matters little: One and Two do remain outside, which offers her a certain feeling of security or a sensation of shuddering, depending on the circumstances, and Laura greets him knowing that One and Two are there outside of the apartment (what apartment, really?), right there on the other side of the so-called door, maybe just waiting for him or guarding him, and sometimes she can imagine that they keep her company, especially when he looks at her fixedly, as if trying to conjure up the memory of things out of her past that she doesn't share at all.

Sometimes she has violent headaches and this pain is the only intimacy that she is able to share with the man. Later on he remains aloof, absent, anxious and fearful that she might somehow remember something out of her past reality.

The concept

She is not insane. She feels certain about this although at times she asks herself—and even Martina—where she gets the notion about this idea of insanity and at the same time this confidence of being sane. But at least she knows this much, she is sure that it's not a matter of having eluded reason or understanding but rather a general state of forgetting the past, which does not feel unpleasant at all. It's rather soothing.

This so-called anguish is something else: this anguish bores into her stomach and makes her want to cry with her mouth closed, more like a sigh. She says—or thinks—the word *sigh* as if she could see an image of the word, a clear-cut image in spite of the fact that one single word can't be too clear. It remains an image that is—must be, it couldn't be otherwise— filled with memories (where did the memories go? Where could they have gone knowing more about herself than she did?). Something existed in the back of her mind, and at times she tried to extend an invisible hand to take memory by surprise and catch it, something really quite impossible: impossible to reach into the corner of her brain into which her memory seemed to have retired. That is why she finds nothing: her memories are blocked out, fenced in.

And when she is making love with the guy he suddenly looks at her as if he wanted to extract these memories from her or rather as if he saw in her an imbedded past that she can't manage to raise to the surface of the present.

There definitely lurks about a time that existed before this house and before the great nothing; a time that existed before Martina and even before this man who claims to be her husband.

The photo

There on the night table stands the photo to prove it: she and he looking into each other's eyes with a nuptial glee. She is wearing a veil and an ambiguous expression behind the veil. He, however, is basking in the triumphant awareness of somebody who got what he wanted. Almost always when she gets a good look at him he adopts this triumphant mien of those who believe that they have made it in life. And then suddenly, it all vanishes, as if somebody threw a switch, it's gone and the triumph turns into doubt or something more opaque, something difficult to explain, something unfathomable. That is to say: open eyes that lowered their lids, hermetic eyes staring at her and not seeing her, or maybe only seeing what she has lost along the tortuous route from the past to the present; that what has remained behind and will never be recovered because deep down the last thing she wants is to recover it for herself. But there remained the realization that she had walked along that route filled with all its obstacles and detours and that this route belonged to her.

This existing in a vacuum, in an everlasting present, in a world that is born each moment or at the most was born a few days ago (how many?) is like living in a cotton cocoon: soft and warm but without any texture or taste. But also without harshness. She has been little exposed to harshness in this very soft and slightly pinkish apartment where Martina only talks in a murmur. But she knows intuitively that this harshness exists, especially when he (Juan, Martin, Ricardo, Hugo?) squeezes her too hard and it becomes more of a hate-filled stranglehold than an embrace expressing love or at least desire, and she suspects that there is something unknown behind all this, but this suspicion does not even reach the level of a reasoned thought, it is but a spark crossing her mind and there it all ends. Then all returns to softness, to a letting-herself-be, and once again the beautiful hands of Antonio caressing her, his long languid arms wrapped around her body holding her close without oppressing her.

The names

Sometimes Juan appears to be very handsome, especially when lying spread out next to her.

She calls him "Daniel, Pedro, Ariel, Alberto, Alfonso," with a soft voice while guiding her hand over his bulging muscles and inhaling this smell that reminds her of herbs.

"More," he demands, and one doesn't know whether he says it because he likes the caresses or the succession of names.

And then she offers him more of each, and it seems that she baptizes each zone of his body, even the most intimate ones. Diego, Esteban, Jose Maria, Alejandro Luis, Julio and a stream of names that fails to dry up, and he is showing a serene smile that somehow lacks sincerity. Behind that mask something crouched lies ready to pounce at the slightest trembling in her voice as she pronounces a name. But her voice continues on the same note, without any emotion or hesitation. It's as if she were reciting a litany: Esteban, Francisco, Adolfo, Armando, Eduardo, and he can submerge himself in his sleep and feel for a moment that he is all of these names to her and can assume all of their functions. But the truth is that *all* equal *none,* and she continues reciting names for a long time even though he is asleep, reciting names and pretending to play up to the motionless and saddened wonder of his manhood, reciting names like a mnemnotic exercise done with a tinge of pleasure.

The one with the endless names, the one without a name, sleeps, and she can study him until reaching a saturation point. The one without a name seems to divide his time with her between making love and sleeping, an uneven division: most of the time he sleeps. A feeling of relief is in the air, but relief from what? They seldom talk to each other, seldom do they have anything to communicate: she is not even capable of remembering her earlier life, and he acts as if he knows her earlier life or as if it did not matter to him, which comes to be the same.

Then she gets up carefully so as not to wake him—as if it were easy to rattle him once he decided to give himself over to sleep—and walks naked about the bedroom and sometimes the living room without worrying about Martina and gazes for a long time at the front door with its multiple locks asking herself if One and Two would still be out there, perhaps sleeping on the threshold like a couple of watchdogs, asking herself if they might turn out to be shadows, shadows that could conceivably befriend this strange woman that was herself.

And indeed she feels strange, foreign, different. Different from whom? From other women? From herself? That is why she runs back to the bedroom to look at herself in the big wardrobe mirror. There she examines herself from head to toe: sad nobby knees, few well-rounded curves, and then this unexplainable scar that crosses her back and that she can only see in the mirror by making contortions. It's a thick scar, very noticeable when touched and very recent although it's healed and does not hurt. How did this cut happen to be on this back that seems to have suffered so much? A flogged back. And the word *flogged* that sounds kind of pretty if one does not analyze it gives her goose bumps. Thus she keeps on wondering about the secret power of words, and all in order not to certainly not—enough of this—not to become obsessed again by the photo. She shouldn't and yet she goes back to it, no way out, because it is the only thing that really attracts her in this little warm and yet estranged place. A place that is totally estranged in its pastel-colored tone that she never would have chosen; although, what would she have picked out? Something more indefinite, surely, an artful color like the color of his penis, almost chocolate-brown in its darkness. And in this place exists a personal object that somehow belongs to her less than anything else: the wedding picture. There she stands, very alert and trying to look as absent as possible behind that veil. It's a very thin veil that allows the light to illuminate her face from the outside and accentuate her nose (the same nose that she now looks at in the mirror, that she touches without any recognition as if it had just now grown above her mouth, a somewhat hardened mouth for such a nose).

So what? she asks herself. At least that she can do; say: so what? Be indifferent. She feels too tired to ask herself worn-out questions, and it is truly useless to focus on the dedication in the picture and read half-heartedly:

Laura, I hope that every day will be for us like this most happy day of our wedding. Then comes the signature, extremely legible, Roque. And there is no doubt that it's really she in the picture, in spite of the veil, it's she who is called Laura. And he is Roque. Somewhat hard, granite-like. The name suits him and yet it doesn't suit him; not when he surrounds her with the fragrance of herbs.

The plant

At least she retains the memory of something, and that astonishes her. A happy memory, that's right, one that also contains a bitterness that grows inside of her like a seed, something hard to define: the way memories ought to be. Nothing far-reaching of course, nor too emphatic. Only a tiny little memory that can be lulled to sleep during her insomnia.

It's a plant. That plant in the flowerpot with its leaves criss-crossed by whitish nerves; pretty leaves, ceremonial, darkish, very much like him, really made in his image although Martina bought it. Martina is also dark and ceremonial and likes everything in its place—one leaf to the right, one to the left, and so on—and he was the one who had hired Martina who was made to order for his taste because she, Laura, would have chosen a woman filled with the joy of life, one who sings while sweeping the floor. But he had selected Martina and Martina chose the plant, but only after a long discussion with him, and the plant arrived bearing a single yellow flower, a robust, beautiful flower that luckily began to wilt, which is the lot of a flower no matter how robust and beautiful it may have been.

Martina, on the other hand, did not wilt. She only lifted an eyebrow or maybe both to show her surprise when she called her and said: I want a plant.

Usually the reaction to "I want" came just about right away: I want a cup of coffee, toast, some tea, a pillow; the wanted (requested) thing appeared after a little while without any complications. But to ask for a plant seemingly went beyond the expected, and Martina did not know how to handle that. The poor lady, what could she possible want with a plant, poor sick woman, poor silly thing. And to think that she maybe could have asked for something more substantial and less disquieting, something costly, for instance, although who knows how much anyone would get from this man. Poor locked-up woman, poor fool.

When the master arrived the next day Martina confided to him that the lady of the house had asked for a plant.

"What kind of a plant," he asked, saying the obvious.

"I don't know, she only mentioned the word plant, I don't believe that she has anything specific in mind."

"And why does she want a plant?"

"Who knows. To water it, watch it grow. Maybe she misses the countryside."

"I don't want her to miss anything, it's not good for her. Did she take all her pills? There is no reason for her to think about the countryside . . . What does she have to do with life in the country, I wonder? All right, you go ahead and buy her a little plant if that is going to make her happy, but nothing rustic. Rather a cultivated plant if you know what I mean, and get it at a good florist's."

They were both in the kitchen, as usual, discussing details of the housekeeping that apparently were of no concern to the so-called Laura. But she overheard the conversation without meaning to—or maybe meaning to, trying to find out something, trying without realizing to understand a little more of what was happening to her.

When had there ever been splendor in her life? Was she past such a moment or was it yet to come? These were questions that she formulated in a moment of weakness only to get rid of them immediately because that's not where the real problem lay, the only real problem appeared when she found herself looking at her image in the mirror for a long time trying to find out who she was.

The mirrors

It is a matter of an unexplained multiplication, a multiplication of herself in the mirrors and a multiplication of the mirrors—which is most disconcerting. The last one to be installed was the ceiling mirror, right above the big bed, and he forced her to watch him and herself with open legs facing the mirror. At first she watches out of duty but later with pleasure, and she sees herself up there in the ceiling mirror, spread out on the bed, inverted and distant. She watches herself from the tip of her toes where he is right now drawing a map with his saliva, she lingers over her own legs—without fully acknowledging their existence—her pubic hair, the navel, a pair of astonishingly heavy breasts, a long neck and her face that suddenly reminds her of the plant—something live and artificial—and without wanting to she closes her eyes.

"Open your eyes," he orders, watching her watch herself up there.

"Open your eyes and take a good look at what I am going to do to you because it's worth watching."

And his tongue starts to move up on her left leg leaving a design and up there in the mirror she begins to recognize herself, she begins to realize that this leg is hers because it comes alive under his tongue and suddenly the knee in the mirror also belongs to her and above all the curvature of the knee—so sensitive—and her thigh, and the inner side of her thigh would be hers too if it were not for the fact that his tongue made a detour and dwells on her navel.

"Keep on watching!"

And it's really painful to keep on watching as the tongue keeps on moving up higher and he keeps hovering over her, although he tries not to cover her too much so that she can go on watching in the mirror up there, and thus she discovers the awakening of her nipples, she sees the mouth that opens wide as if it did not belong to her, but it is hers, she feels this mouth, and the tongue on her neck that is still designing her reaches out to this mouth, but only for a moment, without any gluttony, only long enough to acknowledge this mouth and descending again, and a nipple begins to tremble and it's hers, it belongs to her, and down below her nerves tremble as the tongue is about to reach them and she opens her legs wide—they really belong to her although they reacted to an impulse that did not emanate from her consciousness but that somehow did originate in her—in a pleasurable trembling, so close to a sensation of pain just when his tongue touches her erotic center, a shuddering that she would like to postpone occurs as she presses her eyelids closely together, and then he shouts:

"Open your eyes, whore!"

And she feels as if he had torn her to pieces, as if he had been sinking his teeth into her insides—maybe he bit her—as if this cry had twisted her arm to the breaking point, as if he had kicked her head in. "Open your eyes, spill it, tell me who put you up to this," and she shouts a "no" that is so intense, so deeply submerged that it doesn't make the slightest sound and he doesn't hear it at all, a "no" that seems to blow the mirror on the ceiling to pieces, that multiplies and multiplies and cuts up his image although he fails to notice it and so his image and the mirror remain intact, in one piece, and emptying her lungs she utters "Roque," his real name, for the first time, but, impervious to so much inner turmoil, he doesn't hear this either.

The window

Alone again in her habitual state—the other thing was an accident, he is an accident in her life in spite of the fact that she can invent all kinds of names for him—she is alone as she ought to be, quiet and composed. Although sometimes his presence confers a certain purity on her. She sits at the window looking at a sterile white wall asking herself what lies behind the wall and thinking only of him.

The window features a wooden frame painted white and the wall across the window is also white and shows some opaque streaks produced by the rain. She believes that she must be on the sixth or seventh floor, but the picklock is missing and only he can open it, which does not concern her much. She does not care for fresh air and to lean out of the window would only produce uncontrollable vertigo. Suddenly she imagines him walking about the streets with a picklock in his pocket, like a weapon to be put in the fist and slammed into a jaw.

But why does she think about streets and fists at all? The notion of street does not really bother her. However the idea of a weapon . . . a weapon let loose on the street, a time bomb, and he walking this very street and the time bomb or the blow-up coming, and he walking this same dark street and the picklock from the window or whatever it is called, an oval object, almost a bronze egg, and the window here, so obstructive, a window that limits the outlook instead of enlarging it.

The streaks on the opposite wall that hides the sky reveal almost nothing: it is better not even to look at them. He, however, would be able to reveal some truths but he only says what he wants to say and truth probably does not penetrate into her inner chambers. He says what he wants and what he wants is not what interests her. That's the way he is, but then he is also different: there's his way of looking at her when they are together, of wanting to make her part of himself, there is this slow ritual of undressing her, undressing her slowly to discover her in each inch of skin that appears after each undone button.

Once in a while she has an inkling that all this might have to do with what is called love, this indefinite feeling that sometimes expands inside of her like an inner warmth which does not last very long but which on sublime occasions bursts out into a flame. None of this indicates that it has anything to do with love, not even with her sudden desires, desires for him to arrive and caress her. It's just the only way to experience that she is truly alive: his hands caressing her or the voice saying: "Get going, whore. Tell me you are a bitch, a slut. Tell me how the others fucked you. Do they fuck you like this? Tell me how they do it."

Or maybe it's because of this, precisely, because of his voice telling her things that make her feel like being someone else, living other sensations and being another person.

And sometimes she is tempted to tell him: Bring in those two from outside the door, at least that way I can know that there exist other men. But she prefers to keep quiet about such things, at least consciously, because on the other hand there exists this blacked-out zone in her memory (memory?) that is also quiet but not because it wants to be.

The black hole of memory maybe was similar to the window opposite a white wall with certain streaks. He is playing his cards close to his chest, so she isn't going to find out anything, and, really, does it matter? Her only interest lies in being there, watering her plant that looks plastic enough but does need water, applying cream to her face that also feels made out of plastic and looking out of the window at the vast, dilapidated wall.

The colleagues

Then he is there again and something seems to be happening.

"Some friends of mine are going to come by tomorrow for a couple of drinks," he says to her in an off-hand manner.

"Drinks?" she asks.

"Yes, sure. Just a whisky, before dinner, they won't stay long, don't worry."

She is about to repeat the word "whisky" but stops herself in time. A stupid question that covers up the real one: "What friends?" The words escape her just when she was about to shut up, but maybe this way she can clear up something.

And he deigns to answer her. For once he consents to raise his head patiently, answers her question and behaves as if she existed:

"Well, not precisely friends. Three or four colleagues, that's all, just for a little while, a little entertainment for you."

Strange, thinks the so-called Laura. Colleagues, entertainment, a little while. Since when such attention for her? And then comes the really astonishing part:

"Look, I'm going to buy you a new dress. That way you can receive the guests looking pretty and feeling good."

"Is a new dress supposed to make me happy? A new dress is something special?"

Bull's eye! Just the type of questions he can't stand. Better try to remedy this; so she adds: "But I am glad your pals are coming."

"Colleagues," he corrects her with emphasis.

"All right, colleagues. That will make me learn new names, I'll have to address you differently."

"Don't even think about that, all those names are ugly, I don't want to hear them. Besides, once in a while you could make the effort of calling me by my real name, right? Just for a change."

The next day he does show up with the new dress that is pretty all right and obviously also expensive. She looks good, smiling inwardly, and the colleagues with the unpronounceable names arrive all at the same time; they walk in with a sort of military posture and squeeze her hand as they call her Laura. She accepts the offered hands, nods her head to the name of

Laura as if accepting it herself, and his colleagues sit down on the chairs and begin to examine her.

Above all the insistent questions about her health produce a strange uneasiness that she cannot understand.

"Do you feel well now? Your husband told us that you had problems with your back; does your spinal chord hurt anymore?"

And then those chance remarks: "How pretty you are, you have a perfect nose . . . "

And all those questions that disguise an interrogation and begin with "Do you think that . . . ?" And she is conscious that they are talking to her other self, her true self: "Do you think?" And she sitting there trying to answer as best as she can, not wanting to fail in this first examination although she is not quite sure why she thinks about interrogations and examinations, or why the idea of failing or not failing could matter to her at all. And then she accepts a drink—just a short one (don't drink too much, it won't mix well with your pills, he whispers to her almost solicitously)—and she turns her head when someone calls her Laura and listens carefully.

" . . . that was the time when they planted bombs in the Palermo barracks, remember?" one of them said and naturally addressed her.

"No, I don't remember. I really don't remember anything."

"But it happened when the guerrillas were active in the North. You're from up there, from Tucuman, aren't you? You surely remember."

And the one without a name, his eyes glued to his glass, replying:

"Laura doesn't even read a newspaper. Whatever happens outside of these four walls interests her very little."

She stares at the others without knowing whether to feel proud or indignant. The others stare at her too but give no hint of how she should behave.

When the colleagues finally leave after a lot of talking she feels empty and takes off her new dress as if needing to get rid of something in herself. He looks at her with the air of someone who is pleased with his own work. Suddenly she needs to vomit, maybe because of that little bit of whisky, and he gives her a pill that is different from the other ones she usually takes.

One and Two remain outside, as always. She hears them whisper out in the hall. Maybe they escorted the guests to the lobby and now are back; yes, sir, she can hear them and knows they'll only go away when he leaves. And she will be alone again as befits her, until he will show up again so that everything can start anew, one guy inside and two outside, one inside of her to tell the truth and the other two as if they were in there with him sharing her bed.

The well

The times when she makes love to him are the only moments that really belong to her. They belong to her, to the so-called Laura, to this body here—that she can touch—that encloses her, all of her. All of her? Isn't there something else, like being deep in a dark well and without knowing what it is all about, something inside of her, dark and deep, something that has nothing to do with her natural cavities to which he has such easy access? A dark, unreachable recess in her, a center-place, the site of an innerness where everything that she knows is locked in, yet it is a knowing without knowing, and she cradles herself in it, she rocks in her chair, and the black well goes to sleep like a subdued animal. But the animal does exist, it's inside of the well and at the same time is the well, and she does not wish to arouse it because she is afraid of the claws. This poor, deep, black well of hers, so mistreated, so neglected, abandoned. She spends many an hour pulled inside out, like a reversed glove, interred in her own well, in a uterine obscurity that is lukewarm and humid. Sometimes the walls of the well make sounds and it matters little what the sounds mean although every so often they seem to send a message—a lashing—and it makes her feel as if they were applying hot coals to the bottom of her feet, and suddenly she returns to her own surface, the message is too powerful to endure, and then it is better to be out of that black vibrant well, better to form part of the rose-colored room that is supposedly hers.

He may be in the room or not, usually he is not, and so she withdraws into herself; then she smiles into multiple mirrors that return something like a recognition that she firmly rejects.

Then he reappears, and when he shows himself tender and loving, the well turns into a little illuminated hole way down at the bottom; and when he treats her with a nervous harshness, the well opens its abyss-like mouth and she feels tempted to jump in, but she doesn't jump because she knows that the nothingness down in the black well is worse than the nothingness outside.

Outside of the well she possesses the nothingness with him, the one whom appearances designate to be her man. When she is with him and the well becomes a little hole, she spies through it to see him in a minute frame. She observes him through two fine lines that cross in the center. Through the well made into a little hole she looks at him as through a gunsight, and that she doesn't like at all. Which one of the two is holding the rifle? Apparently it is she; he is caught in the square lines of the sight and she looks at him without understanding too well why this should be so and without wanting to find out (she simply refuses). He smiles at her from the other side of the sight, and she knows that she will have to lower her weapon. Lower her weapon and her head: these are things she is getting used to little by little.

The whip

"Look, how pretty," he tells her as he opens up the package. She looks at him with a certain indifference. Until the package reveals an almost immaculate, almost innocent gaucho whip with its thick handle and a wide, short whip, a leather strip made from fresh, raw hide. And she does not know about such things, she has forgotten all about the horses—if she ever had been close to them at all—she starts to scream desperately, to howl as if they were going to cut her to ribbons with the whip or rape her with the handle.

After all, maybe this was just one of his ideas, to bring a replacement for himself. Or maybe he had visions of giving her a good whipping or maybe—why not?—asking her to whip him or rape him with the handle.

The woman's cries stop him in the middle of his unconfessed visions. She is standing in the corner weeping like an injured animal, so it's better to leave the whip for another time. That is why he recovers the paper from the wastepaper basket, straightens it out with the palm of his hand and wraps the whip up again. This way he won't have to hear any more screams.

"I didn't want to upset you," he tells her, and it's as if she didn't hear him at all because the words did not fit him.

"Excuse me, it was a stupid idea."

He excusing himself, that's something hard to imagine, but that's how it is: excuse me, quiet down, purr purr, he says it almost like a cat and the idea of cat envelops her with a warm feeling and somehow stops her convulsions instantly. She thinks cat and moves away from him. From the very corner that has become her refuge she can move towards other boundaries where everything is open and where there is a sky and a man who really loves her—without a whip—so that there can be love. The sensation of love that runs over her skin like a hand, and suddenly this horrible, all-pervasive feeling that the loved one is dead. How can she know he is dead? How can she be so sure of his death if she hasn't been able to endow him with a real face, a complete form? But they have killed him, she knows that, and now it's her turn to firmly carry on with the cause; all the responsibility lies in her hands when all she wanted was to die with the man she loved.

A complex texture of remembrances—feelings invades her through her tears, trembling, and then subsides into nothingness. After the feeling of having been so close to a revelation, a recognition. But it's not worth it to arrive at this state by the way of sorrow, and it is better to remain as before, floating, not allowing the clouds to disperse: the soft, protective cloud that she must retain in order not to be suddenly struck down by memory.

She sobs silently and he runs his fingers through her hair trying to return her to the zone of forgetfulness. He runs his hand through her hair and tells her in a sweet voice:

Don't think, don't torment yourself, come with me, that's the way, don't close your eyes. Don't think. Don't torture yourself (let me torture you, let me be the owner of all of your pain, your anguish, don't try to escape from me. By what is most sacred to you, don't run away from me). I am going to make you happy, all the time more happy. Forget that damned whip. Stop thinking about it. See? We're going to throw it out, I am going to make it disappear so that you don't get any more frightened than necessary.

He slowly moves towards the front door, crosses the living room with the whip (the package with the whip inside) in his hands. He takes the keys out of his pocket—why doesn't he use the other set on the mantelpiece right next to him, she asks herself—opens the door and with a fairly theatrical gesture throws the box out in the hall where it falls making a bland, rubbery sound.

See, it's gone; he is talking to her now as if she were a child. And suspicious like a child she knows that it isn't so, that on the other side of the door stand One and Two, ready to pick up everything that he throws to them, ready to pounce upon the box like preying beasts.

One and Two. She never forgets them, they are always out there although they don't belong in her world. They belong as little to her as those keys on the mantelpiece, present and absent like the whip due to the simple fact that it brought about her overwhelming desperation, something like a dynamite charge.

These then are her explosions, depth charges that explode when least expected due to the action of the detonator. They explode sympathetically, so to speak, vibrating in unison with her, or maybe it's just the opposite: due to a reaction with other vibrations that are let loose.

The truth is that the explosion takes place and she remains disconnected, in the midst of her own ruins, shaken up due to an expanding wave or something like that.

The peep-hole

It is not a new sensation, no, it's old and comes from far away and from earlier times and from submerged zones. It's almost a feeling, a strange knowledge that only manages to upset her: the notion of a secret. And what can that secret be? Something known to her and yet something that has not surfaced. Something very deep and forbidden inside of her.

She tells herself: this happens to everybody. But even this notion perturbs her.

What can this forbidden (repressed) thing be? Where does the fear end and the need to know begin or vice versa? The price of knowing the secret is death itself; what can this hidden thing, this far-reaching depth charge be? Wouldn't she be better off not even acknowledging its existence?

He helps her sometimes by refusing to help her in this task. By not helping her, he is actually lending a hand in opening her inner doors.

Wanting to know and not wanting to know. Wanting to let herself be and at the same time not wanting. More than once he gave her the opportunity to look at herself in the mirrors and now he is about to offer her the frightening chance of seeing herself in the eyes of others.

He undresses her slowly in the living room and the moment comes. She can't quite explain to herself how she knew it from the very start—maybe it was the fact that he was undressing her in the living room instead of the bedroom. He reclines her on the couch that faces the front door and begins to undress himself without uttering a word in a silent ritual that is meant for other eyes. And suddenly he moves away from the couch, walks naked to the door, uncovers the peephole—that tiny rectangular piece of bronze—and leaves it up. Just like that, without any rhyme or reason. But then he hesitates, he really hesitates before turning around and moving again in her direction as if he hated to turn his back to the peep-hole and would rather face it, pointing at it with his imposing erection.

She cannot distinguish anything on the other side of the peep-hole but she senses them, she can almost smell them: the eye of One and the eye of

Two glued to the peep-hole looking at them, knowing what is about to come and drooling in anticipation.

And he approaches her slowly, brandishing his darkish penis, and she cowers in a corner of the couch with her legs drawn up and her head held between her knees like a trapped animal, but maybe that's not it at all: not a trapped animal but a woman waiting for something to unravel in her, waiting for the man to come quickly to her side and help her with the unravelling, and she wants those two outside to help her too, offering a single eye to this emotion that shudders through her body.

The mating game begins to get cruel, intricate and overly lengthy. He seems to be trying to cut her in half with his thrusts and then stops in the midst of a gurgling sound, only to penetrate her again with fury, impeding her movements and sinking his teeth into her.

At times she attempts to escape this maelstrom that carries her away and tries hard to discover the eye behind the peep-hole. Other times she forgets about the eye, all the eyes that are gathered together out there, anxious to watch her twisting body, but he shouts one single word—bitch—and she comprehends that he uses this term as a focus for those watching from the outside. Then a long sigh escapes him in spite of himself and he quickly redoubles his thrusts so that her moans can be transformed into howls.

This means that outside there are not only eyes but also ears. Not only One and Two are standing outside but also certain colleagues of his.

What good are those eyes, ears, teeth, hands to the ones who are on the other side of the door and who cannot break through the obstacle? And because of this obstacle he keeps on penetrating her with fury and without pleasure. He turns her over, he twists her body, and suddenly he stops, lifts his body and stands up. Then he starts to pace the floor like a caged beast, displaying the vitality of an unsatisfied male animal, roaring.

She thinks about the crowd outside that is observing—looking at her—and so she calls him back to her side in order to cover her with his body, not to satisfy her physically. She wants to use his body to cover her up as if it were a pillow case. A body—not her own, never her own—that can serve as a screen, a mask, to face the others. Or maybe a screen to hide from the others, so that she can disappear forever behind or under another body.

Yet, what for? Hasn't she disappeared a long time ago? Those on the other side of the door only have that small peep-hole to get at her.

Communicate with them? Impossible, and then an intuition, a

nebulous feeling rises in her, telling her that she can transmit her human warmth to the others—those outside—only through another person, through the one who is only here to function as a bridge leading to the others, the ones on the outside—only through another person, through the one who is only here to function as a bridge leading to the others, the ones on the outside. Tired of roaring he returns to her side and starts to caress her in an unexpected change of heart. She lets the caresses invade her and fulfill their mission until her whole nervous system responds to the caresses, and the vibrations caused by the touch gallop through her blood stream and finally explode.

The two bodies then remain inertly on the couch and the peep-hole darkens as if it now lacked the lucidity of a human eye.

After a while Martina enters quietly and covers the two bodies with a blanket.

The keys

Later on he leaves. He is always leaving, when she sees him, he is turning his back to her and moving towards the front door, and his real goodbye is always the noise of the key that closes the exit, leaving her again on the inside.

She is no longer deceived by those keys, the other ones, those on the mantelpiece next to the door: without having tried them out she knows that they don't fit the lock, that these keys are lying there as a kind of trap, a lure, and if she would ever dare to touch them all hell would break loose. That is why she does not get close to them in spite of the temptation to stretch out her hand towards them and even talking to them as if they were friends. These poor keys are not to blame for setting up an ambush for her. More than once she has caught him glancing at the keys as he came in in order to make sure that they were still in the same position in which he had left them. The dust settles on these poor keys, Martina aims a little at the keys with her duster as if they were made out of some delicate crystal.

When leaving he also checks if the keys are in the proper place not far from the door lock that they couldn't open anyhow, and then he closes the door and turns the lock twice with the real keys and leaves her—the so-called Laura—free to submerge herself again in that dark, timeless well.

The voices

Only the sound of the clock exists, the rhythmic tic-tac of the clock . . .

and it seems to be almost a living thing. Almost a living thing and yet not quite real, no real voice calls out to her to save her from herself.

He calls her enough all right. His voice shouts the name of Laura enough times, once in a while from afar (from the other room) and he shouts it into her ear while on top of her, calling her because he feels like it, imposing his presence—also hers—and the obligation of being there just for him and ready to listen.

It's always the same with him: Juan, Mario, Alberto, Pedro, Ignacio, whatever his name is. No point in changing his name because the voice is always the same and so are his demands: to be with him but not too much. He requires a non-entity, a pliable being that he can shape according to his will. She feels like a piece of clay, soft and changeable as he caresses her; and yet she doesn't want to be that, she refuses to be soft and changeable, and her inner voice screams with fury and bangs on the walls of her inner being while he is recreating her according to his whims.

Every so often a rebelliousness flares up in her that has a close relationship with another feeling: fear. Later she feels nothing; it's as if the tide had ebbed away leaving a wet, smooth beach in its wake.

She roams freely and barefoot on this wet beach trying to shake off the horror experienced at high tide. So many breakers covering her yet never cleansing her head. The waves come in and then retreat leaving a salty and sterile scum on which only a sort of undefined and reduced terror grows. She roams the wet beach and at the same time she is the beach—her own beach, her own stagnant waters—and so she is not made of clay but wet sand that he also wants to shape following his own whim. All of her has become wet sand so that he can build sand castles like a kid, creating his illusions.

Sometimes he uses his voice to guide her and calls her by her name and calls out the parts of her anatomy in an obscure attempt to rearrange her.

This is the voice that sometimes calls her and that cannot penetrate her shell. Afterwards comes the smile: his somewhat forced smile, and only when he laughs—on those very rare occasions when he does—something undesirable seems to awake in her, something tearing at her insides that has nothing to do with laughter.

So she really has little enough motivation to leave her dark well and rise to the surface. She doesn't want anything to reach her from the outside, except that at that very instant the bell rings insistently, something unusual that suddenly brings her to the here and now, and somebody desperately tries to make himself heard, and then he cautiously approaches the front door to see what the matter is and she in her nervous, alerted state hears other voices without understanding them.

"Colonel, a thousand pardons. Colonel, there has been an uprising and it seems that the third infantry regiment has joined them. So has the Navy. It's an open insurrection. Excuse us, colonel. We didn't know how else to reach you."

He gets quickly dressed and leaves without the slightest goodbye as he has done so often. But he is indefinitely more hurried and maybe even forgot to lock the door. But that is all. The rest, the voices outside remain a usual and disturbing sound, nothing else, maybe because she can't or won't decipher anything. Interpret these phenomena? What for? Why try to understand things that lie beyond her meager capacity of comprehension.

The secret (secrets)

She suspects—without wanting to make it too clear to herself—that she is about to find out what she should not know. She has been afraid of these deep-seated secrets for so long that they have become inaccessible and don't even belong to her anymore.

At times she would like to seize secrets and dig around a bit, but it is betterr not to, better to leave them be: in the stale waters of an unfathomable depth.

And then she begins to crave for food and constantly asks Martina for a cup of coffee with milk, biscuits, fruit, and Martina must be thinking: this poor woman is going to lose her figure eating and eating and never moving around or getting any exercise. And the master is gone.

But neither Martina nor she mention the master's extended absence. She doesn't want to—or can't—remember the voices she heard when they came for him. Martina had been at the grocery store and never knew anything.

Martina used to take advantage of going shopping when the master was in the house and now she can't decide whether to leave this poor insane woman by herself, wait another day or leave for good. The master had left her with enough money to allow her to be on her own, and maybe by now he got tired of this game and it is up to her to leave in time and forget the whole affair.

But these problems belong to Martina, not to the so-called Laura who doesn't even leave the bedroom any more but lies stretched out on the bed spending the day in pursuit of some vague sensations.

She repeats the word *Colonel* to herself but the word only produces a sharp sensation in the pit of her stomach . . .

Much later, almost a week later, he finally returns and yanks her out of a dream in which she saw him walking on the deep waters of the secret without getting engulfed by them.

"Wake up," he tells her as he shakes her. "I have to talk to you. It's about time you found out."

"Found out what?"

"Don't play dumb. You heard something the other day."

"It didn't mean anything to me . . . "

"That's all right, it doesn't have to concern you, but I want you to know anyway. Otherwise you'll just be in between."

"In between?"

"In between."

"I don't want to know anything, leave me alone."

"What do you mean, leave me alone. What's that about not wanting to know? Since when do you give orders here?"

"I don't want to know."

"Well, you're going to know everything. Much more than I had planned to tell you at first. What's all that nonsense about not wanting to know? There'll be no secrets for you, like it or not. And I'm afraid you won't like it at all."

She would like to put her hands over her ears, cover up her eyes, put her arms up to her head and crush it. But he opens the little suitcase that he brought with him and takes out a purse that attracts her attention.

"Remember the purse?"

She shakes her head vehemently but her eyes tell a different story. Her eyes become alert and alive after all this time of opaqueness.

"Look at the contents. Maybe it'll shake you up a bit."

She puts her hand in the purse but withdraws it right away as if she had just touched the viscous skin of a toad.

"Go ahead," he encourages her, "put your hand in the purse and take it out."

Something in her head shouts a big No. Her body begins to shake desperately until she bangs it against the wall. She just wants to keep on hitting the wall.

But he knows how to handle the situation. He slaps her face and barks his command: "Pull it out, I'm telling you!"

And then, more quietly: "It doesn't bite. It doesn't sting you. It's an object without life. Only you or I can put life into it if we want to. And you no longer want to, isn't it true you no longer want to?"

"I don't want to, I don't want to," she moans.

In order not to repeat the performance (the head banging against the wall and the slap in the face) he puts his own hand into the purse and pulls out the object. He holds it in the palm of his hand where it looks so harmless.

"Take it. You ought to recognize this gun."

She stares at it for a long time while he holds it out to her until she finally picks it up and begins to examine it without really knowing what it is all about.

"Careful, it's loaded. I never go around with unloaded arms, even when they don't belong to me."

She raises her head and looks at him with a premonition of knowledge, almost at the edge of what could well be her own abyss.

"Don't worry, sweetie. Now you know and I know. You might say we are even."

The word *no* repeats in her mind and makes her shake her head. This is not the way to be even, not with this revolver between us.

"Yes," he cries, and it's almost a howl. "We can never reach an understanding if you remain locked within yourself refusing to know. It was I who saved your skin, do you know that? It may not seem like it, but I did save your life because they would have finished you off like they did with your boy friend, your accomplice. So you better listen and snap out of your pretty little dream world."

The revelation

. . . and his voice begins to pound away and keeps on pounding: I did it to save your skin, you bitch, all the things I did to you were done to save you and you have to understand that so the circle becomes complete and my work is done, and she feels like a ball of yarn pressed against the wall noticing a drop of paint hardened on the wall, and he insisting it was I, I alone who did not let them touch you, I alone, there with you, hurting you, depleting you, mistreating you to break you like they break a horse, break your will, transforming you, and she glides the tip of her finger over the drop of paint as if nothing happened, as if thinking about something else, and he insisting you were mine, all mine because you had tried to kill me, aiming at me with that same revolver, remember? you have to remember, remember, and she thinks about the friendly drop of paint, so tender to her touch while he goes on I could have cut you into little pieces, but I only busted your nose when I could have broken every bone in your body, one by one, your bones that belong to me, all of them, have done anything, and her finger and the drop of paint became a single unit, a common pleasurable sensation, and he going on and on, you were a piece of shit, garbage, worse than a whore, they caught you when you were aiming at me looking for the appropriate angle, and she lifts her shoulders, not because of him or what he is saying but because a little drop of paint refuses to respond to her or to modify itself, and he all wrapped up in himself, you didn't know me but you wanted to kill me anyhow, you had orders to kill me and you hated me although you didn't know me, hated me? so much the better, I would force you to want me, to depend on me like a new-born babe, I also have my weapons, and the little drop of paint containing dried-up tenderness was still connected to her and beyond it the smooth, impenetrable wall, and he going on without changing, repeating: I also have weapons.

The denouement

"I'm awfully tired, stop telling me stories, don't talk so much. You never talk that much. Come on, let's go to sleep. Come to bed with me."

"Are you out of your mind? Didn't you hear me? Enough of this nonsense. Our little game is over, get it? It's all over for me, and that means it's also over for you. Curtains. Get that through your head because I am taking off."

"You are leaving me?"

"Naturally. Are you expecting me to stay? We have nothing else to say to each other. It's all over. But thanks anyhow. You've been a good pet and it was fun at that. So now come to your senses and everything will be all right."

"Stay with me. Come here, go to bed."

"Don't you realize that this can't go on? Enough already, get a hold on yourself. The fun is over. Tomorrow morning they'll unlock your door and you can leave or stay, spill the whole story, do whatever you please. At any rate, I'll be far away by then . . . "

"No, don't leave me. Aren't you ever coming back? Stay."

He shrugs his shoulders and, as so often before, turns on his heels and walks towards the front door. She looks at his slightly hunched back that is moving away from her and she feels that the fog inside of her is clearing a little. She begins to understand a few things; she understands above all the function of the black instrument that he called gun. Then she lifts it and takes aim.

CECILIA ABSATZ

Cecilia Absatz was born in 1943 in Buenos Aires where she studied for several years in the College of Liberal Arts at the University. From 1965 to 1973 she had been active in the advertising field. From there she went into publishing and is now general editor of the magazine *Status,* billed as *Revista Masculina,* a magazine for men.

Her only book of fiction to date is a collection of stories called *Feiguele y otras mujeres* (1976). This volume contains two distinctly separate sections: the first one deals wit6h the growing pains and frustrations of a fat, Jewish teenage girl who must fend for herself against pitiless treatment from her peer group. In the second part of the book the author reveals a most skillful use of irony as she focuses on the women and men belonging to the local professional scene. It is noteworthy that the portrayal of female-male relationships in stories like "A Ballet for Girls," included in this anthology, shows a complete abandonment of the traditional "Latin" moral code for women as they treat sex with a casual indifference that might belong to the ambiance of a singles bar in New York or London. On the other hand, Feiguele, her family, and friends, belong to the social context of the large Jewish community existing in Buenos Aires which gives this city a multi-ethnic and cosmopolitan quality.

BIBLIOGRAPHY

Feiguele y otras mujeres, 1976 (stories)

A Ballet For Girls

Cecilia Absatz

"Come along with me," said Irene, "let's drop in on a friend's party."
And so I followed Irene passively and got into a taxi.

It was Saturday night in the big city and the traffic rush was on. In the taxi Irene went on with her story about Alejo almost shouting because the driver had a soccer game going on the radio.

The story was very typical for Irene: it turned out that her present romance with Alejo amounted to what she called a practical affair, certainly of therapeutic value; and the fact that he was married and had three children did not matter that much, and considering all the angles, everything seemed to be under control.

"Maybe on Tuesday I'll manage to drag him to Martha Peluffo's grand opening and you'll get a look at him. I'll want you to say exactly what you think of him. Because at times I look at him and then ask myself 'who is this guy anyway?' . . . Sometimes I just get a little spaced out because, at times, this guy is true blue . . . I'll tell you, there's a big shortage of men with a heart—she sighed—if things don't improve we'll have to turn lesbians all the way. Good Lord, listen to that radio (somebody had just scored an impossible goal) . . . Irene's finger with its red-lacquered nail touched the driver's shoulder. "Mister . . . "

"Huh?" The driver turned his head and looked at Irene's knees.

"Be a sweetheart and turn that thing off," she purred into his ear, "I hate noise."

2

We went up in a glass-covered elevator and got off on the top floor. The bell sounded very musical and right away a maid took us inside.

155

I sat down in an armchair covered with white silk and looked around: in this place everything had been done in black and white except for the plants. I would not have been surprised if suddenly an orchestra had started to play, the doors and ceiling disappeared and a group of girls dressed in gauze appeared from behind the curtain and began to dance a ballet.

"The host is an architect?" I whispered to Irene. The carpet loomed white and very thick. I spotted a collection of exotic vases and an original Vasardy on the mantelpiece above the fireplace framed in black iron.

"The hosts are both architects," Irene corrected me. She managed to fit perfectly into the color scheme that would be all shot to hell if the maid turned out to be a redhead.

The Handsome Architect suddenly made his appearance, dressed in white, from behind an enormous dog, naturally also in white.

He approached us wearing a marvellous smile and sporting a penetrating look that is exclusive property of handsome men and that penetrates the eyes of a woman, collects his image and returns to him.

To tell the truth, the architect did look handsome. And if that did not make a real impression on me (which remained to be seen), it certainly impressed him.

A little later his wife, the Elegant Architect, made her grand entrance . . . She was the kind of woman who would always dress in beige. She was also the kind of woman that would always manage to look impeccable, no matter how many hours she had put in at work or how rough the going had been. As soon as I saw her I knew that she would eat by taking tiny little bites and suppress her sneezes. The drinks and canapes were being passed around (and then it was time to verify the first of my two hypotheses: it took her two bites to eat the tiniest petit four).

Everybody seemed absolutely charming, and the conversation flowed with an elegance commensurate with our professional backgrounds. The humor was subtle and the wit penetrating for the benefit of those who love subtle humor and penetrating wit, like me, for instance.

The chimes sounded again and two new guests walked in: the Energetic PR Woman and the Intelligent Psychoanalyst. The newcomers slid into the conversation as if they were getting under silken bed sheets.

The Energetic PR Woman spread her perfume and unfolded her wings: she sat on the knees of the Handsome Architect and never forgot to throw a secret kiss at her young husband while at the same time making a pass at me.

The Intelligent Psychoanalyst on the other hand talked in a guarded tone and his style was rather laconic. Whenever he made a comment it was expressed with great brevity and always meant to explain something. I believe that it will not be necessary to give a verbatim account of the ensuing conversation and so I will just present a list of the topics:

1. The brand-new pregnancy of the Elegant Architect.
2. Children in general.
3. Psychoanalysis for children.
4. Psychoanalysis in general.
5. Sensitivity sessions.
6. Group sex in general.

Here I must point out that at no time was this vulgar expression mentioned under point 6. The words used proved to be far beyond my meager knowledge and my poor memory could not reproduce them now. But I am still sure that the talk dealt with group sex.

The glasses kept on being refilled and the party became more lively. Stretched out on the carpet next to the Intelligent Psychoanalyst and the Elegant Architect, Irene was holding forth. I hate to admit it, but I was trying very hard to unsettle the Energetic PR Woman by responding to her overtures with a mixture of childish gestures and ardent looks.

The Handsome Architect changed imported records, served drinks and dropped *bon mots* all over the place.

Everybody kept on talking. Completely plastered, Irene concluded her stimulating conversation with the Intelligent Analyst exclaiming: "I don't give a damn what anybody says, I just don't like to suck any cocks."

This affirmation had occurred during a rare moment of silence and made everybody realize that it was time to go home.

The Handsome Architect offered to drive us home, and Irene and I accepted gladly.

"You don't talk much, do you," he addressed me directly for the first time after Irene had been dropped off.

"No, I generally don't," I replied. We kept on driving in silence.

"Why?" I asked after a while.

"That's a strange question."

"That's not an answer to my question."

"I never pretended that it was."

"Why do you refuse to answer me?"

"Why are we fighting like this?"

"We are not fighting at all!"

"No?"

New silence. The Architect stopped the car at the curb of an unknown street and turned off the engine.

"I don't like to fight," he said, "I hate violence."

"Why?"

"That's a surprising question."

"I find it interesting."

"You are not against violence?"

"No."

"No?"

"No. How can I be against violence. That would be like being against my nose."

"That's pseudo-intellectual talk."

"Or rather, what I don't understand doesn't exist."

"How's that?"

"Oh, nothing."

"Are we fighting again?"

"Not any more."

New silence.

"You sure don't say much."

I did not answer him.

"I know that you don't like me, but at least I irritate you, and that's something."

I smiled.

"Am I doing okay?"

"So far."

"Why do I irritate you?"

"Because you are very obvious."

"What does that mean, I'm very obvious? You hardly know me."

"Your place is very obvious too."

"My apartment? You didn't like it?"

"I liked it a lot, it's like the home of all the other architects I have known."

"I get it. And your apartment?"

"My place reflects myself."

"I want to see it."

"All right."

He started the car and drove to my place. We did not say anything in the elevator and avoided looking at each other. When I opened my door and switched on the light I thought that my apartment looked more beautiful than ever.

He glanced at it from the threshold and only said: "May I come back tomorrow?"

"Of course," I answered.

"I'll be here at ten o'clock." He turned around and left.

3

At ten o'clock sharp on Sunday night the buzzer rang. I let him in. The Handsome Architect appeared in my apartment impeccably dressed, combed, shaved, shoes shined and cologne on his cheeks. I would have been really glad to see him if it had not been for the fact that he made me feel more like a client than a hostess.

He took my glass of whisky and sat down on the couch. I have to admit that he managed to be the first person to look quite uncomfortable on this couch.

The couch in question is enormous and upholstered in brown velvet, one of those pieces of furniture from which nobody wants to get up once seated. It is a couch that equals a mother's arms. The happy combination of a soft back and the arm rest forms a hollow spot that suggests refuge and friendship. Its proportions are those of a generous lover and its faint smell envelops one like childhood remembrances. To lean into this couch is like diving into the sea. Yet, the Handsome Architect sat down on it as if it were a pointed stone.

"Why don't you make yourself comfortable," I tried.

"But I am comfortable."

I put on a record, offered food, more whisky. I felt like a mother whose son had come home to see her out of a sense of duty.

Finally I left him alone.

Suddenly he asked me: "Have you known Irene long?"

As can be imagined, I did not answer right away; not only was this a very direct question, but it promised to start a fascinating conversation.

"Do you really want to know how long I've known Irene?"

"Oh, I get it," he said. "A difficult woman."

"Uh huh."

He began to look around a bit, the whisky glass glued to his hand. "Nice clothes rack."

"Yes, very nice," I said.

At precisely what point do people start making love? Does anybody know?

I am sure that it begins much earlier than the act of lovemaking. It starts suddenly while making small talk or discussing a big issue, or not speaking at all, but thinking intensely, eating maybe, or looking at each other, or listening to music, maybe when picking a hair off the jacket of the other person, discovering each other in a mirror, an elevator mirror, each one talking about himself or herself; anyhow, it starts long before taking off one's clothes.

The Architect, handsome as all getout, did not make love. At least not to me. He showed a deep interest in the clothes rack, objects in general and my TV antenna in particular.

I kept on bothering him with all kinds of offers (more whisky, cake, pot) when it suddenly happened: I found a pair of lips on top of mine.

After a process of quick elimination I concluded that the lips had to belong to the Handsome Architect, and then I started to tremble.

I began to tremble because I knew the agenda: 1) mouth to mouth resuscitation, 2) tit grabbing (only one though), 3) peeling off the clothes. No deviations allowed.

I thought rapidly. What do I do? Meanwhile step one continued and step two could not be far behind. What should I do? Stop the whole thing right now?

And that led me to thinking about the type of conversation that would inevitably follow if I stopped step one. Could I possibly stand the boredom?

So I decided that the most practical solution would be to go ahead with it: all I had to do was to remain still and wait. It could not possible take more than five minutes. Then he would leave and that in itself would bring about a happy ending. Besides, to be frank, there remained a remote glimmer of hope that the Handsome Architect would surprise me at the last minute and produce some unexpected magic.

No such luck. The next five minutes turned out to be the most boring ones of the whole day.

After some horizontal gymnastics—to give the thing a name—the

Handsome Architect got up and retired to the bathroom. That gave me a chance to change the record and sip some coca cola.

After a while he returned and started to get dressed in a sort of absent-minded fashion.

When he had finished he walked over to the television set and tested the antenna.

Then he said: "With this inside antenna you don't need an outside one, do you?"

I thought this one over for a minute. Clearly such a question required a certain amount of thought.

"No," I answered finally, "with this antenna here I don't need one outside."

REINA ROFFÉ

Reina Roffé belongs to the younger generation of Argentine women writers. Born in 1951 in Buenos Aires, she studied humanities at the University of Buenos Aires and then proceeded to forge a career in the world of newspapers and magazines that put her in close contact with the national scene. While she often interviewed such famous figures and Jorge Luis Borges or Victoria Ocampo, and published a book on the well known Mexican writer Juan Rulfo, she felt always attracted to the problems facing the modern Argentine woman. She headed the women's supplement in the newspaper *La opinión* and presently is a feature writer for the magazine *Bazar,* where she has a page dedicated to women's life.

In 1973 she published her first novel, *Llamado al Puf,* which won first prize in the Sixto Pondal Rios contest. Three years later she came out with her second novel, *Monte de Venus.* The book won immediate critical acclaim, especially from other Argentine women writers, but the military government banned its sale three months later. Reina Roffé had dared to portray Argentine women outside of the stereotyped roles that fit into the rigid male minds of the censors. The narrator of the first half of the novel is a young lesbian who possesses the will power to endure a picaresque existence amid the disapproval of society-at-large and the selfishness of her lovers in particular. The second half of the book is centered around the activities of a group of young women who attend an evening school to obtain a needed high school diploma. Representing a cross-section of urban lower middle class, the girls display a fierce spirit of independence

163

that culminates in their efforts to seduce some of the male teachers and to defy the school authorities as *Peronismo* comes to power briefly for a second time. No doubt the double dose of female aggressiveness and the attack on traditional conventions was strong enough to shock conservative minds.

Lately Reina Roffé has continued her literary career by writing a number of short stories, while attending the International Writers' Workshop at the University of Iowa with a Fulbright grant in 1981. One of these stories, "Let's Hear What He Has to Say," has been written expressly for this anthology and remains unpublished so far in Spanish. It is a work representing the new female awareness of the Argentine woman writer of today.

Llamado al Puf, 1973 (novel)
Monte de Venus, 1976 (novel)

Let's Hear What He Has To Say

Reina Roffé

*The Woman is incredibly more evil than
the Man and more secretive; goodness in
the Woman takes on a form of degeneracy
. . . the struggle for equal rights is truly a
symptom of illness; any physician
knows that.*

Friedrich Nietzsche

*The ball bounces back from the wall right into my racquet and I hit
it even harder, back and forth in some sort of frantic action. Parks can be
so desolate when the wind dies down and shows their empty benches. I
like it when once in a while a couple sits down on a sun-flooded bench to
talk and the little man goes on like this for instance:* If that is what you
want, go ahead, go far away and don't ever turn back, until the earth
swallows you up, or even better yet, until you sink into the mud made up of
earth, rain and the leftovers of your feeble brain. I had other plans for you.
I wanted you to soar, be free, be yourself, be somebody, somebody big and
strong and outstanding, somebody worthy of the attention of others, of
those who would desire you. I like it when other men desire and love you,
and when other women envy you, follow in your footsteps and look up to
you as their leader. I have known it for a long time, in fact I have always
told you: the day would come when your chains had to fall off and you
could see for yourself what's what, but . . . at the price of smashing my
head in, throwing me into the garbage can and covering me up with your
little daily triumphs so that nobody can see me? Your memory is really
well controlled, you filter out everything that does not fit into your plans or
that conflicts with your impulses. Have you conveniently forgotten that
you were nothing but a bundle of nerves before you met me, a strange

creature unloved by her father and mother and persecuted and tortured by a perverse brother; and you straining for hours on the toilet seat trying so hard to think about what to do with all your resentment, impotence and furor . . . you sure never got very far! You were going around in circles, blind as a bat, tied to an unhappy childhood, lost on the merry-go-round of your psychopathic gallops. Have you forgotten the times that I ran after you on the street to grab you by the arm before you could throw yourself in front of the first car passing by and thus once and for all finish your agony, all along wearing the rigid expression of the incurable patient, playing the violated maiden, never knowing what it meant to give your life a meaning? Everything was a living hell for you, nobody understood you, nobody had offered you anything outside of aggression and rejection, the very same rejection that you absorbed in order to use it on others and finally on me, on the one person who had hoped to guide you, who loved you more than anyone else, who was stupid enough to cater to all of your whims and whimperings while you were playing the poor, forlorn, capricious baby doll, that sad, misunderstood creature that had to be nurtured along. The things I had to endure, all by myself, without complaining, like a true macho, yes, like a macho, although I know that the term bothers you now since you are running around giving yourself airs of a liberated woman, swallowing all that garbage about feminism. Just go away, beat it, and don't come back.

Now the ball jumps across the ground. I don't feel like picking it up. Yet I am intrigued by this solitary game that dominates my spirit. Swish, bang. In the meantime, my mind operates on two levels and I cock an eager ear. Swish, bang. And the little man goes on almost breathlessly: Let me refresh your memory. I must have talked to you a thousand times, but you never listen, you only hear what is of interest to you so you can take advantage of it. You were a good pupil, and I was a fine teacher, patient and generous to a fault. Do you think that another man would have let you go and be psychoanalyzed, three times a week, let you enter the University and elect a career that would help you to become a professional liar, an accomplished cynic, a therapy-happy charlatan who is nothing but a big fake . . . and to think that I took you to the clinic because I believed that the analysis sessions would do you some good, help you to re-evaluate your past, digest your resentment, assume the role of a true woman, become a worthy social being, yes worthy. You know something? I was and am a real feminist, I took off your chains, I made it possible for you to be free, to soar, so you would not have to be condemned to scrubbing kitchen floors and playing the dumb, tear-jerking housewife. But you took it all too literally. Lately you could not even stoop so low as to sew a miserable button on my jacket or bother about dinner. While I had to fry myself a couple of broken eggs and swallow them like poison, you were putting on airs of a *grande dame* living it up in bars that Virginia Woolf wouldn't have been seen dead in, and running around with your new friends, all divorcées, manhaters, lesbian amateur poets and assorted strange birds of a feather. And you make fun of me behind my back. You ridicule the man who waited a whole year for you to make up your mind what with your hysterical fear of losing that precious virginity of yours. You said you did not want to betray your little old grandmother and your mummy and daddy who had brought you up and loved you, as if they ever did. It took you a whole year to make up your mind and then, what a laugh, I had to shoulder the blame for having been the butcher who stuck the knife into you and shed your blood all over the sheets, not exactly blue blood like in the fairy tales, and then had to look at the tears, crocodile tears shed for the shed blood and the irreparable loss. But all that was nothing compared to what happened afterwards. I had to wait and wait burning up like a candle until you finally learned to relax your body and mind and come at the right time, because when I didn't or couldn't wait you madly accused me of being selfish. And for starters there had to be those endless foreplays, linguistic preludes that left my tongue in worse shape than a worn-out piece of shoe leather, and, oh beware, if your moans didn't fill the room, the building, the neighborhood or all of Buenos Aires. You needed cries of glory that amounted to nothing but hysterical sobs. And to think I did it all for you, I was the feminist, I was the exception, the only one who really loved you.

It is such a delight to hit the ball to the proper spot, compulsively, violently, feeling the vibration of the racquet, like words properly directed to make the right impact, while the tennis ball creates a brief shadow before hitting the wall, and the little man continues: Let's see now, who encouraged you to go out and look for a job? Who told you that you should earn your own money in order to become independent, gain self-esteem and buy whatever you wanted without feeling guilty, debased or hurt in your pride? Who revealed to you that money equals power? What? But you not only wanted to be equal to me, you wanted to be different. I don't understand you. Well, now you are working and making more money than your mentor. Does that make me feel inferior? Well, damned, of course it does. But never mind, I made you over, I taught you all there is to know; read this, don't read that, don't waste your time on the other. I created a sense of urgency in you, the realization that life is short and that we just have time to do a few things right. And, of course, I created a monster. And so you started to tell me: No sir, I refuse to be the workhorse that comes home from an eight-hour job to play housewife. You forced me to take care of my clothes, to dry the dishes, wash my coffee cup. I, who had never done any of these things in my life, did them to help you, to make you feel better, all along sharing those abominable tasks. Remember, do you remember when I had to turn off the TV in our bedroom so you could read leisurely until midnight, your filling the apartment with more and more books until every corner was filled with stacks of them, and your going on with that reading spree without ever considering whether I minded that light and your silence, until you finally decided to sleep on the little couch in the living room and leave the bed to me? Yes, all right, I know you moved so as not to hear me complain anymore, leaving me to my TV and the soccer games, et cetera, et cetera. But in the meantime I had to grin and bear it, tired of all your ups and downs, your problems without solution, and the compromises that you finally came up with and that always worked in your favor although you protested that they applied to the both of us. You always knew how to take advantage of every situation, good or bad, doing your thing while saying all along that it was for the good of the both of us. Don't make me laugh, for the both of us? For you and nobody else but you, for the perfect individualist, the perfect narcissist, who wanted to squeeze the last drop out of every day, every occasion. You wanted it all! And to think that I thought I could change you, that my love would change you, that it was only a matter of giving you time to become a mature person, to get rid of all that confusion in your mind so that you could understand how important it is to have a home and a man who protects you, who takes care of you, and who sacrifices himself for you. I was willing to give you all the time in the world and wait for the right breaks. Just tell me, where else could you find a man with such patience? You want to be alone now? Live by yourself? Let's see, let's just see how that is going to work out. The truth is that you really don't know a damned thing about life because life isn't at all the way your novels describe it, nor the way your girlfriends paint it, those frustrated females who have ruined you. Do you know what happens to those women who live by themselves? If you could only see them . . . cocksure of themselves during daylight and crying their hearts out in the dark of the night. They jump from one bed into the next one. Perfect freedom. Baloney! Freedom is just another form of slavery. Those women are consumed by that precious freedom of theirs. It makes them bitter, like pure vinegar. The years roll by, age catches up with them, and when they finally realize that and want to change their lives it is too late. They are old and lonely; nobody even wants them anymore. They have nothing to offer anybody, not even to themselves, no children, nothing. Oh wait, I know what you are going to say, that children and a man aren't everything. Yes, you can run after a hundred different things, but in the end none of them turn out to be as important as they seem at first. I don't know why I take the trouble to keep on talking. You need to have your own experiences, and that's what you really want, isn't it? That's what all you women want, right? That's what you have been looking for all these years, right? But always secretly, when my back was turned, lying to me, never saying a word, always having that long silence, those constant excuses while I was sitting there never knowing what you were thinking or scheming. And one day you had the nerve to tell me that I could never understand you because I was a man. Now that is sexual racism, and more than that, it's sexual discrimination, cheap feminism. Mine is the true feminism. Sure, there are times when I hate all women, when I hate you. All of you are of inferior, poor stock, small-time revolutionaries, charlatans who read a few books and memorize some pamphlets, pocket-size Evita Perons. All of you are greedy for power to make up for your penis envy. That's it, penis envy, because you are condemned to go through life castrated.

The ball seems tired after so many rebounds and starts rolling across the hard and naked ground over into the grass. I quickly run after it but that puts me out of range so I can't hear the voice. Thus it is up to me to recreate the final fragment of the monologue as well as the answer of the girl who by now is walking downhill, sure of herself, never turning her head back to look at the darkish figure of the abandoned little man, still seated on the park bench, stirring a few pebbles with his foot and staring at the reddish dust that is slowly settling on his leather boots. No doubt he told her: All right, I admit my mistakes. I'm only human. I have my own problems, but at least I solve them myself, without involving others, without making other people feel guilty or responsible for my conflicts—if I have any. I don't blame anybody for my despair—it does take over a lot of times—because I feel marginal too. Who doesn't feel alienated in this society? Believe me, nobody. And that is something you women can't see. You don't see that because you are sick and engaged in a struggle without objectives, without knowing what you will get out of it, and so you are left alone like stylish puppets that have gone out of style. All of you women could achieve something much more vital and valuable. But you would not be happy that way, nothing can make you happy, you are eternally dissatisfied, you deny everything that sounds reasonable, you just keep on searching and searching, and what are you looking for? For me to leave you, to tell you to go away and never come back; that way you wouldn't have to feel guilty or thank me for what I did for you, as the old tango lyrics put it. See how I make things easy for you? Even now at the very end. That is what I call being big-hearted, something you don't know the meaning of. Take it easy. I do wish you luck. At any rate, I know that you will never be able to forget me. I was the first man in your life. I have fashioned you. You are made in my likeness and image. *That was when she said:* Haven't you heard that God is dead?

Biographic Note on Translator

H. Ernest Lewald first became acquainted with River Plate culture while attending a high school in Montevideo and working for a newspaper in Buenos Aires. In the United States he studied French, German and American literature before finally deciding on a doctorate in Spanish. Although his dissertation dealt with Spanish nineteenth century naturalism, he began to publish articles and, later, books on Spanish American literature and culture. He is presently chairman of the Latin American Studies Department, The University of Tennessee.

Motivated by his multicultural experiences, Professor Lewald has long had a strong interest in the "relativistic" aspects in literature influenced by the Argentine writer Jorge Luis Borges and the Mexican Carlos Fuentes. He further focused on reflection of the rapidly changing values and behavior patterns in Hispanic societies. This line of inquiry is reflected in his works: *Buenos Aires: retrato de una sociedad hispánica a través de su literatura* (Houghton Mifflin, 1968), *Argentina: Análisis y autoanálisis* (Sudamericana, 1969), *The Cry of Home: Cultural Nationalism and the Modern Writer* (University of Tennessee Press, 1972), and *Latino-américa: sus culturas y sociedades* (McGraw-Hill, 1973).

During his frequent visits to Argentina, Professor Lewald has come to know many outstanding women writers, and his more recent publications examine the woman's interpretation of River Plate society. The present volume of translated stories represents a logical sequence to his interest in the literature of social change and offers a point of view that has not often been available to the American reader.